DADDY'S LOST LOVE

LAYLAH ROBERTS

DADDY'S LOST LOVE

Laylah Roberts

Laylah Roberts.

Daddy's Lost Love.

Cover Design by: Allycat's Creations

Editing: Celeste Jones

❀ Created with Vellum

LET'S KEEP IN TOUCH!

Don't miss a new release, sign up to my newsletter for sneak peeks, deleted scenes and giveaways: https://landing.mailerlite.com/web-forms/landing/p7l6go

You can also join my Facebook readers group here: https://www.facebook.com/groups/38683042506991/

BOOKS BY LAYLAH ROBERTS

Doms of Decadence

Just for You, Sir

Forever Yours, Sir

For the Love of Sir

Sinfully Yours, Sir

Make me, Sir

A Taste of Sir

To Save Sir

Sir's Redemption

Reveal Me, Sir

Montana Daddies

Daddy Bear

Daddy's Little Darling

Daddy's Naughty Darling (in the Dirty Daddies Anthology)

Daddy's Sweet Girl

Daddy's Lost Love

Haven, Texas Series

Lila's Loves

Laken's Surrender

Saving Savannah

Molly's Man

Saxon's Soul

Mastered by Malone

Men of Orion

Worlds Apart

Cavan Gang

Rectify

Redemption

Redemption Valley

Audra's Awakening

Old-Fashioned Series

An Old-Fashioned Man

Two Old-Fashioned Men

Her Old-Fashioned Husband

Her Old-Fashioned Boss

His Old-Fashioned Love

An Old-Fashioned Christmas

WildeSide

Wilde

Sinclair

Luke

The Hunters

A Mate to Cherish

A Mate to Sacrifice

PROLOGUE

1
0 years ago

HE CUPPED her head between his hands, staring down into her beautiful face. He might only be nineteen. She might only be sixteen, but he knew what he wanted. . .her.

"I'm gonna call as much as I can." They were at their special place. The pond on his grandfather's estate. It was where they always met. Only tonight was different, because they were saying goodbye before he went on deployment overseas for nine months.

It was going to be hard leaving her. Knowing how tough she had things back here with her shit mother. Taking care of her brother and sister. But he was doing this to build a life for them. Oh, he knew his grandfather would set them up. But Jed was his own man. He wanted to start life with Daisy right.

"I know," she whispered. Tears shimmered in her deep gray eyes.

"I love you, Daisy-girl," he told her.

"I love you too."

"Here, I got you a birthday present." He reached into the duffel bag he'd brought with him, pulling out a box wrapped in pale green paper. Her favorite color.

"A present? For me?"

He loved that she treated every gift she received with a sense of wonder. Hated it too. As he knew she'd received very few in her life.

"I know your birthday isn't for a few weeks. I'm sad I'm gonna miss it. Open that now."

She ripped off the paper like an eager toddler at Christmas, making him laugh. Then she looked down at the box of fairy lights with excitement. "Oh, Jed."

"Know how much you like pretty lights."

"Oh, I do. Thank you!" She threw herself at him and he caught her tight, breathing her in.

"Also got something else for you and you're gonna take it. No arguments." He pulled an envelope out of his pocket and placed it in her hand. "I've put some cash in there for you in case of an emergency."

She opened her mouth and he placed his finger over it. "I said no arguments. It's all mine from working that part-time job over summer. It's for you. I know things might get tight and I won't be here to help. So you put this where your mom can't find it and you use it if you have to. Yeah?"

Her eyes shimmered bright with tears.

"Yeah. Thank you."

He kissed her again.

Sugar and strawberries.

"I'll be home soon. Any trouble, you go to Grandfather. He'll help."

She stiffened next but he felt her nod. She and Grandfather didn't get on well, but Grandfather knew how much Daisy meant to him. He'd take care of her.

1

It was a pretty sad testament to her life that all her belongings fit in the back of her car.

Wasn't even like she had a big car. Just a small hybrid Toyota. It was racy looking and cute, with enough space to fit two suitcases and a couple of boxes on the backseat.

Daisy sat in her car, staring up in wonder at the gorgeous house in front of her. Two-storied with a wrap-around porch, well-kept grounds and obviously freshly-painted, it looked enormous. And far too good a place for her.

Worthless white trash.

She took a deep breath and pinched her thigh until the pain washed away the awful voice in her head. She wasn't trash. She was smart. She was loved. She was worthy.

She banished the bad thoughts from her mind. She could live in this beautiful house. She deserved to. Didn't she have as much right as anyone else to have something like this in her life? She was a good person. She wasn't mean. She didn't kick puppies or make faces at babies or cheat on her taxes.

It was big for one person. She was kind of surprised she could afford it. She'd thought maybe the photos of it had been photo-shopped because it was too good to be true.

But she could definitely settle in here. She worked from home; she wanted a place she could feel happy.

She pulled her cell out of her handbag. She was a few minutes early to meet her new landlady, so she might as well take the chance to text her sister. She sent off a brief message, telling her she'd arrived. Then she took a photo of the house and sent it as well. She'd email her brother later. Not that he'd reply for a while. He was backpacking around Chile and often didn't get in front of a computer.

Sylvie would take a while to reply. If she did at all. Daisy breathed through a ball of hurt at the distance that seemed to only be growing between her and her siblings. She'd basically raised them. She loved them.

But she wasn't going to live her life for them anymore. They were both adults. It was time for her to do something just for herself. She'd needed to get away from the city and, she was ashamed to say, her sister. She loved Sylvie, but she was sucking her dry. She could work from anywhere and she'd always loved the idea of living in a small town. Somewhere with friendly locals and beautiful scenery. She'd done some searching around and found a rental ad for this house. Something had pulled her towards it.

Now here she was.

A truck pulled up behind her, dragging her from her thoughts. Nerves fluttered in her stomach. A man emerged from the driver's side. Holy hell, he was enormous. Tall and broad, with a beard, he took a moment to study her car before moving around to the passenger door of his truck. Her sporty little car looked like a toy next to his enormous double-cab truck. He opened the passenger door then reached in and lifted out a woman who looked to be around the same age as her. She was small with waves of crazy, dark hair.

Daisy watched as the man, who looked like he could bust knee-caps for a living, gently set her down, handling her like she was made of the most delicate glass. He pulled her jacket closer around her then zipped it up. She didn't know if she'd ever seen anything sweeter in her life. Tears welled in her eyes and she had to blink them away.

What she would give to have something sweet like that in her life.

Be thankful for what you have, Daisy.

She looked back at the couple, surprised to find them staring at her car, waiting.

Oh shit. Taking a calming breath, she climbed out of her car. She shivered as a cool wind lashed at her, and she reached in to grab her jacket, pulling it hastily on.

"Um, hello," she called out, hoping she was hiding her nerves. "Are you Ellie?"

"Yep," the other woman said cheerfully. "I sure am. You must be Daisy, then."

Daisy nodded, unable to get any words past her lips as she grew closer. Jesus, this guy was even bigger up close.

Just because he was enormous and intimidating looking, didn't mean he was a bad person.

"Yes, nice to meet you," she finally managed to find her voice and her manners as she held out her hand. Ellie took it into her gloved one, pumping it gently. When she let it go, Daisy turned bravely towards the behemoth who just stared down at her solemnly.

"Hi."

He nodded. Without a word, he reached out and grasped hold of her hand. His was bare, like hers, but much warmer and rough with calluses.

"This is my boyfriend, Bear," Ellie said cheerfully.

"Bear?" she asked startled.

"It's a nickname," Ellie explained. "Due to his size. Plus, he's just a big ole teddy bear."

Daisy sent the other woman an incredulous look.

Teddy bear, right. And she was Goldilocks.

She glanced up at Bear who showed no real reaction to his girlfriend's proclamation that he was just a teddy bear, was staring down at her hand which was still held in his big paw. She snatched it back, feeling herself blushing. What was wrong with her hand?

"You should be wearing gloves," Bear said suddenly. "Hands are freezing."

She blinked up at him. That was why he'd been studying her hand? He thought she should have gloves on? That was strange...she couldn't remember the last time anyone had ever cared about whether she was dressed for the elements. It made her feel warm inside and a little odd. She didn't know this man, why would he care?

She shoved her hands into her pockets and took a step back. She needed to say something to get this conversation back on track, and make her feel less weird. She turned to Ellie.

"I thought you'd be old."

Awesome. Good job, Daisy.

Ellie glanced up at Bear, who was still staring at her strangely. What the hell did he find so fascinating?

She fought the urge to hunch her shoulders, to try to protect herself from whatever he could see.

White trash.

No. She wasn't.

"Um, Daisy?" She glanced up to find both of them staring at her. But not like they thought she was crazy. Rather they looked concerned.

"Sorry, did you say something?"

"Are you all right?" Ellie asked gently. "You looked kind of scared."

She forced her shoulders back. "I'm fine. Sorry, long trip."

They didn't look like they bought her lie. Shit. Then Ellie nodded. "I know what that's like. I drove long hours to get here from Miami then when I arrived, it was snowing and I crashed my car." She smiled up at the behemoth. "Bear rescued me."

There was such adoration in her voice that it made Daisy's teeth ache. And her gut hollowed out with longing. Especially when Bear's face warmed as he glanced down at Ellie. His whole face changed. Grew softer. This was why Ellie was with someone who could snap her like a twig.

Because he absolutely fucking adored her.

And that was something most people searched for all their lives.

"That's how you met?" She found herself asking, despite her usual rule of not getting involved in others' lives or business.

"Yep," Ellie said cheerfully. "He nursed me back to health in this rustic old cabin. Treated me like a princess. It was the first time anyone had ever taken care of me. I was used to being the one who did everything for everyone else and suddenly here was this big, bossy, sweet man ordering me to rest and making me meals and even reading to me."

"Wow." She stared up at Bear. He did not look like the type to sit and read bedtime stories to anyone.

"Yep." Ellie hugged his arm. "Makes a real sexy nurse. Bossy, though."

Bear just snorted.

"This was actually my aunt's house. I inherited it from her. *She* was old," Ellie said helpfully.

Daisy blushed at the reminder of her rudeness. "Sorry, I didn't mean that the way it sounded. Sometimes I just blurt things out without thinking."

Ellie waved her hand around with a smile. "I wasn't upset. I promise the house is all updated and beautiful inside."

"Oh, it looks beautiful on the outside as well. Too gorgeous for me."

Shoot. When would she stop her mouth from running?

"Of course, it's not!" Ellie protested as Bear gave her a funny look.

Crap. Time to get things moving and get them out of here. Obviously, her rusty social skills were not up to talking to people.

"Maybe you should show Daisy around while I carry in her stuff," Bear suggested.

"Oh, you don't have to do that," she protested. "I don't have much. I can get it in later." Although with the way her body ached from long days in her car, she might save the majority of it for tomorrow. All she needed was her blankie, PJs and toothbrush. Even the coffee maker could wait.

"I'll get it." He ran his gaze over her car. "Unlocked?"

"Umm, yes," she said hesitantly as he strode to the trunk and opened it, hauling out her two heavy suitcases out as though they weighed nothing. He started carrying them towards the house without another word.

"Just go with it," Ellie advised on a whisper as she followed him. "He likes to feel useful."

"Right."

Ellie gave her a grin. "Some of the men around here are a bit old-fashioned. There's no way they'd ever let a woman carry something while they're around."

"There's still men like that?" she asked.

Ellie nodded solemnly. "Oh yes. And thank goodness for it."

"Ellie!" Bear called out.

"Oh right, I have the key. Come on," she said.

When Daisy walked into the house, she was struck by wonder for a moment. Bear carried her suitcases up the staircase. She knew she should protest. After all, it was her stuff and he was being a bit high-handed. But she would have struggled to carry her suitcases upstairs. So, she took the opportunity to instead study the inside of the house with its gleaming wooden floors, high ceilings, and wainscoting.

"Like it?" Ellie asked.

"Like doesn't even come close," she whispered.

"Oh goody." Ellie clapped her hands just like an excited toddler, surprising a smile out of Daisy.

"I'm glad it's furnished, it's huge." How was she going to heat it? What would she do rattling around on her own in these big rooms? What was she thinking?

"I'm so glad you're going to be living here, Daisy," Ellie told her, taking her hand.

"You are?"

Ellie nodded. "I know it sounds silly, but the house was lonely and none of the other applicants felt right. Before I met Bear, my aunt was the only person in my life who cared about me. I don't want to sell her house, but I also don't want it sitting empty. Sometimes it feels like she's looking out for me and when I saw your application, I think she guided me to you."

She gaped at the other woman. Ellie blushed lightly. "You think I'm a total whack job, don't you?"

"Who called you a whack job?" Bear rumbled as he walked down the stairs. He glared at Daisy who immediately stepped back, her hands held up.

"Not me, Mr. Big Bear," Daisy said quickly, biting her lip as Bear stared at her incredulously.

Ellie giggled as she went bright pink. "I said it about myself," Ellie finally told Bear, letting Daisy off the hook.

Bear just pointed at her with a stern look on his face. Ellie seemed to understand what he was silently saying and nodded, as she tried to stifle her giggles. Then he looked over at Daisy, shook his head and muttered something to himself as he headed back out the door. Presumably to cart in more of her stuff.

"I cannot believe I just said that," Daisy groaned, placing both hands over her face in mortification. "I'm gonna go hide now. I can never see him or you ever again."

Ellie tugged her hands away from her face, looking up at Daisy from her shorter height. "Well, that's a shame seeing as I was going to invite you out to the ranch for a cookout."

"You live on a ranch?" Daisy's embarrassment faded slightly at that. She'd always loved animals. And she had plenty of authors she edited for who would love some more insight into the way a ranch worked.

"Uh-huh, Bear works at Sanctuary Ranch which is about an hour's drive from here. We live on the ranch. It's gorgeous and this weekend, we're having a cookout. Would you like to come?"

Go to a cookout with a bunch of people she hadn't met? That sounded like a form of hell.

You came here to settle down. Make friends. Meet people. Can't do that staying at home.

Shit. Shit.

Be brave, Daisy.

"Daisy? You don't have to be scared. I'll be there. I'll stay with you the entire time. I just thought it might be a good way for you to meet people. But if you'd rather not go—"

"No, no, I'd like to. Thank you. I'm just a bit shy around strangers."

Ellie smiled. "You don't have to worry, everyone on the ranch is awesome. I'll give you directions out there."

Bear walked in, carrying her laptop bag and a box of linen.

"I just need a piece of paper to write down the directions to the ranch," Ellie said.

"Directions to the ranch?" Bear asked, sending first Ellie, then her, a look. And that look said he was none too happy about what he was hearing.

He didn't want her there?

"I invited Daisy to the cookout this weekend," Ellie explained, seemingly oblivious to the fact that her man looked less than enthusiastic at that news.

"Ellie," Bear rumbled.

Ellie frowned up at him. "Daisy doesn't know anyone here; the cookout is a good opportunity to meet people."

Bear's eyebrows rose. "You know how Clint feels about strangers on the ranch."

"I think he'll be fine about Daisy coming."

"It's okay," Daisy said. "I don't have to come. I mean, I have lots of unpacking to do and I've got work and stuff. Thanks anyway."

Chicken.

Bwok-bwok-bwok.

Both of them turned to look at her.

"Really. I don't want to get you into any trouble," she reassured Ellie.

"Oh, I'm used to getting into trouble," Ellie said with a wink. "Makes life more interesting, right?"

Not in her experience, no.

"Besides, Clint just likes to grumble but he's a big softie underneath."

"Big softie, huh?" Bear said. "I'll tell him that."

Ellie didn't seem worried at the threat. "Please come, Daisy. Really, I'd like you there."

She glanced over at Bear, but he didn't offer up any more protests.

"If you're sure," she said quietly.

"Of course, I am. Tell you what, why don't I get one of the boys to come pick you up," Ellie suggested.

"Ellie," Bear said again. More silent conversation went on between the two of them.

"That's okay," Daisy told her. "I'd rather have my car with me." In case she needed to make a quick getaway. Besides, she didn't want to have to ride around with some stranger. Urgh.

Ellie looked disappointed for some reason, but then she plastered a big smile on her face. "I'll text you the directions to the ranch if you like. Let me know when you're gonna arrive so I can meet you at the gate."

Bear just sighed.

"Now, let me show you around a bit. We put in central heating so you don't need to worry about lighting the fire."

Daisy followed after Ellie, listening carefully. She was making a new start at her life and she wanted it to be perfect.

"So, you want to tell me what that was about?" Bear asked as he pulled the truck away from the curb.

"What?" Ellie asked with false-innocence.

"Pretending not to understand is akin to lying in my book and you know where that will get you, don't you, little girl?"

She stuck her lower lip out in a pout. Damn, she was beautiful, his girl. His love. His woman. His Little.

He reached over and took her hand in his, giving it a light squeeze, ever mindful of his strength and her delicateness.

Not that she wasn't strong in her own way. She had a core of strength that amazed him. But she was his to care for. And Bear was a big guy. He'd never want to do something to harm his girl.

"Ellie," he warned. "Tell me what's going on, unless you'd like to spend the afternoon lying on your stomach in bed with your red-hot ass on display."

"Hey, you can't spank me for being nice."

"Course not," he grumbled. "I'll be spanking you for being a brat and not answering me when I ask you a direct question. Spill it."

She sighed. Long and dramatically. He had to bite back a smile. Damn, she was too cute. He could think of a number of different ways he'd like to spend the afternoon. With his mouth between her legs for a start. Then having her ride him. And then he'd do her hair up into two high ponytails and give her Little some play time. With Daddy watching over her closely.

"I'm not sure what you mean, I was just being friendly."

"Ten."

She turned to glare at him. He just glanced at her briefly before turning back to the road. He didn't want her to sense his amusement. That would send the wrong message. This was serious. It wasn't like her to hide things from him. He liked that she was an open book. Of course, she only thought she was keeping something from him. He was pretty sure he knew exactly what was happening.

"Why is it ten? I didn't do anything," she complained.

"Why'd you invite a stranger to the cookout?"

"I was just being friendly. Daisy is my tenant and she doesn't know anyone. She seemed lonely."

He'd give her that, the other woman did seem very alone. And he'd felt bad about leaving her. But she wasn't his responsibility, even if she was their tenant.

"She did," he agreed. "But she's not part of Sanctuary, Ellie."

"Neither was I. But I am now."

"Because you're mine, little girl."

She glowed at those words. "I am. And Daisy might be someone else's."

He sighed. It was just as he'd expected. "You're matchmaking."

"Well, you can't deny that there are a whole lot of single men on Sanctuary who need a woman of their own and Daisy might just fit the criteria they're looking for."

He shook his head. "You can't know that she's a Little or a sub. That she'd want a relationship like the ones that happen on Sanctuary."

"You mean you didn't get that vibe off her?"

"Ellie," he said sternly. "We met her for five minutes. You can't know. And you got no business inviting her to Sanctuary without checking with Clint first."

"I can't have friends over?" she asked quietly.

"You know that's not what I mean," he replied. Concern filled him. "You lonely, baby? If you need to get off the ranch more often or if you have needs that I'm not meeting then—"

She reached over and placed her hand over his mouth. He pulled them carefully off the admittedly deserted road. Still, he wouldn't take the risk of being distracted while driving. Especially when carrying around such precious cargo.

He turned to look at her and she dropped her hand. She shook her head, staring up at him with such love in her expressive eyes that his breath caught in his throat.

"Oh, Bear. I don't need anything or anyone but you. There isn't a need you haven't met. Usually, you figure them out before I do. I love you so much."

"I want you to be happy."

"I am. I promise. I love living on the ranch. I have amazing friends, a wonderful home and a gorgeous, loving man. There's nothing more I need. I just. . .Daisy looked kind of sad. On her own. And I got the feeling that what she had in her car was all that she owned."

Yeah, he'd gotten that feeling too.

"She had this lost look in her eyes. I get what that feels like. You rescued me. I wanted to help her."

"You got a kind heart, baby girl. But not everyone can or wants to be helped. And I don't want you getting hurt."

She smiled. "You'll protect me."

He leaned in and kissed her. "Always. But you're telling Clint about inviting her."

"What? Can't you do that for me?" She stared up at him with wide eyes.

"Nope."

"But you're supposed to protect me."

He snorted. "Clint ain't gonna hurt you and you know it."

"His lectures hurt. He gave one to Eden the other day that lasted two hours."

Bear just shook his head at that. Then he started up the truck again and pulled out onto the road. "And you're still getting those ten."

"A scolding and a spanking? Sheesh, that's what I get for trying to be nice?"

"Nope, it's what you get for trying to keep things from your daddy."

"I just want everyone to be as happy as we are."

He gave her a look. "Ain't no one as happy as I am to have you."

2

"Coming to the cookout?" Kent called to Jed as he strode out of the gym and down the passage towards where Kent stood with his woman, Abby. His muscles burned, sweat slickened his skin and he was about as relaxed as he ever got.

There was still no damn way he was going to some cookout.

"Nope."

Kent quirked a grin.

"It will be fun," Abby, Kent's woman, spoke up. "Charlie is doing most of the cooking. I promise Ellie hasn't been anywhere near the food." She smiled up at him. She was a sweet thing. Perfect for Kent. He'd never seen his boss this happy.

It was kind of sickening. And he was jealous as hell.

First Bear then Clint now Kent. Everyone was falling like flies around him, finding gorgeous women to love and cherish and discipline, while he...

Would never have that.

"Ellie's even invited her tenant," Abby offered hesitantly. "She said she's really lovely. Doesn't know anyone around here."

Kent gave her a stern look. "You and Ellie aren't matchmaking, are you?"

Abby's eyes widened. "Matchmake her with Jed? No." Then as though she'd realized how what she'd said might sound rude, she turned her gaze to Jed. "I'm sorry, I didn't mean that the way it sounded. . .I just meant, well, Ellie said she's real quiet and shy. And I mean, you would be ill-suited with her, right? That's not your type, your type would be. . ." she trailed off.

"Rambo Barbie?" Jed offered, knowing his nickname.

"No," Abby squeaked. "Oh Lord, help me."

"Dug yourself a big ole hole there, sweet girl," Kent said with a sigh.

"I'm so sorry, Jed. I didn't mean to be rude."

And he knew she hadn't been. Just as he knew that he had done nothing to put her at ease around him. He didn't have much patience for social niceties. It was no wonder they all called him Rambo. All he'd ever cared about was the job.

"If you don't want to come, I'll bring you up some food," Abby said quickly. "Of course, by the time I get it up the hill, it will probably be all over the floor of the truck. . ."

"I'll come," he said abruptly.

"What?" She blinked, staring at him. Even Kent looked shocked. Considering how he treated any social get-together in the past as more painful than being stabbed in the eye, he got their incredulous looks. But he also couldn't have Abby feeling bad, or worse, trying to bring him up some food.

"I'll come," he growled again. "Just don't make a big deal out of it."

"Sure. Okay. See you there!" She smiled big.

He just shook his head and stomped away. She was going to make a big deal about it. He just knew it.

~

SHE HAD no business being here.

Stupid. Stupid. Stupid.

She needed to leave. Just turn her car around and head back to her house in Russell.

Except it's not your house. Your belongings fit into the trunk of your car. You have nothing.

You are nothing.

No. That wasn't true. She was something. She wouldn't let that asshole's words get to her. She was loved. She was smart. She was Daisy.

Not nothing.

She took a deep breath and pulled out the sucker in her mouth. It was nearly gone. She crunched on it. Hopefully, the sugar would help with the jitters that were making her hands shake. She looked around, unable to see Ellie anywhere. As instructed, she'd parked her car in front of the huge, imposing gates.

Sanctuary Ranch.

Nice name. She doubted it lived up to its promise, though. No such thing as a sanctuary. Well, once she'd had it. In Jed's arms. It was the only place she'd felt safe. Loved. At peace.

She took a deep breath. Let it out. She had to move on. She knew Jed had. A few years ago, she'd made the stupid decision to go searching for information about him. Only to discover he was engaged. To a gorgeous, classy brunette. They would be married by now.

She pressed her hand to her stomach as though there was a gaping wound she was trying to heal. She should never have gone looking. It hurt too much.

No doubt his grandfather approved of her. At least that old bastard was dead now. Her brother had sent her his death notice eight months ago.

Yes, it was definitely time to start a new life. Make a place for herself.

Headlights approached.

No going back now, Daisy.

HE KNEW it was a bad idea as soon as he arrived. This was not his scene. He'd just eat some food, drink a beer and head back to his cabin. Alone. Jed walked towards the tables that were laden with food. Charlie must have been prepping for this for days. He grabbed a plate, and started to load up.

"Hey, Jed."

He looked over at the greeting and nodded at Charlie as she walked closer to the table and started rearranging dishes.

"Charlie. Good spread."

Her smile flashed like a beam of light across her face. "Thanks. I wasn't sure if you'd come, especially after Abby put her foot in it. I mean. . .um. . .I'll just shut up now."

He raised his eyebrows with a sigh. Obviously, Abby had told her friends about their conversation. Clint came up behind Charlie, putting his arm around her waist. "Thought I told you to sit down and put your feet up. You're so exhausted you're swaying."

Jed studied Charlie under the lights that had been strung through the trees. She did look tired.

"She's been working non-stop for days to prep all of this," Clint grumbled. "Next year, you're going to enlist some help."

"Oh, so there's going to be a next year?" Charlie teased. "Last night you were grumbling that this was never going to happen again."

"That's because when I woke up at one this morning to find that instead of sleeping beside me, you'd waited until I fell asleep to sneak out of bed and go down to the kitchen to make some more potato salad. There's enough potato salad here to feed Napoleon's army."

Jed had to agree with that.

"Hmm, now that I think about it, I guess there's a reason that you don't want to sit, huh?" Clint asked her.

Jed had to hide a grin as Clint squeezed her ass and she squealed. She'd obviously received a spanking for her disappearing trick. Well-deserved too. That was his woman, his Little, she'd find herself tied to the bed for the rest of the night.

Or secured in a cot.

He let out a sigh. He'd tried to repress his Daddy Dom side over the years. He'd played at clubs with subs, some of them Littles. But he'd never had a Little who was his. His fiancée hadn't been into the lifestyle. Getting engaged to Jennifer had been a mistake. He'd gotten involved with her to please his grandfather. When he'd realized how ill-suited they were, he'd ended things.

"Looks like Ellie's visitor is here," Clint grumbled, pulling him from his thoughts. The other man was scowling as he stared at someone behind Jed.

"Clint, be nice," Charlie told him. "Ellie said she doesn't know anyone."

"Yeah, and I know nothing about her. This is my ranch. Up to me to look out for everyone here. What if she's a serial killer?"

Charlie sighed and shook her head. "Your brother runs a security agency. He has a bunch of deadly bad asses working for him, are you really worried about one woman?"

"I'm not worried," Clint argued back. "And I've learned never to underestimate a woman. All I'm saying is that if I start letting people invite whoever they like to the ranch then soon Eden's going to want to bring back all her crazy friends. And if one of them slaps my ass, you might go into a murderous rage and kill them. I'm just trying to save you from a jail cell."

Charlie and Jed stared at him incredulously. Then Charlie

burst into laughter. Jed shook his head. People round here were crazy.

Strawberries and sugar.

He grew tense at the familiar scent.

"Hey guys, can I introduce you all to my new tenant? Clint, Charlie, Jed, this is Daisy."

Lots of people had that name. Didn't mean it was her. He turned. Stared at her. It was like a sucker-punch to the gut. He couldn't talk. Couldn't breathe.

"Hello, Clint, Charlie, thank you for having me."

Her gaze turned to him. He couldn't see the color of her eyes in the dim light, but he knew they were a deep gray. Her hair, when he'd known her, had been long and straight, now it was cut shorter into more of a bob. She'd always described her hair as plain brown, but she was wrong. There was nothing plain about her.

His eyes wandered down her body. She'd always been thin, but she might be even thinner now, he thought with a frown.

She sucked in a sharp breath. "J-Jed?"

He didn't answer her.

"Is that you?"

"You know Jed?" Ellie asked.

"Um. I used to. Long time ago."

Ten years. Ten years since he'd heard her voice.

"Really! That's awesome," Ellie said cheerfully.

No. It wasn't. He still said nothing. Everyone started to realize he wasn't reacting with enthusiasm.

Daisy cleared her throat. He recognized the sign of her nerves. She hugged herself. Nervous and uncertain. Somewhere deep inside him, feelings unfurled. He'd pushed them deep. Locked them away. But her presence awakened them.

The need to protect. To take command. To care for.

"Jed. How are you?"

"Fine," he snapped. Why was she here? This couldn't be a coincidence, no matter how she was playing it.

His Grandfather's warnings came back to him, about how all sorts of people would come out from the past, wanting something from him when they realized he'd inherited a fortune. He'd never wanted his grandfather's money, had always wanted to go his own way. He'd thought Daisy had understood that.

Until she'd left him. With just a note telling him that she could no longer wait. That she needed to get out of that town. That she'd fallen in love with Bobby-John Jones, the biggest dick in the county. That last bit wasn't in the note, that was just his view of BJ.

His grandfather had told him back then that he'd always thought Daisy was with him for the money, that she saw him as her ticket out of her life. Had she searched him out now because she'd heard about his inheritance?

"Good. That's good."

"Wow, this is awkward," Clint commented.

"Clint," Charlie scolded.

"Well, it is. Obvious that they more than knew each other. Look at that body language and how tense they both are. Question is, would they rather tear each other's heads or clothes off?"

"Clint!" Both Charlie and Abby protested this time. And Jed realized this couldn't happen with an audience. Especially not around Clint, who was the nosiest, most interfering bastard on the planet. And he had a warped social filter.

"We need to talk. Alone," he told her.

He put his plate down on the table and gently but firmly grasped her wrist and tugged her behind him towards the tree line.

SHE DIDN'T PROTEST as he tugged her along. Her stomach bubbled with nausea. How had this happened? How was Jed here? Was he no longer in the Navy? Was his wife here with him? She studied him as they walked. The boy she'd known had been the promise of this man. He'd been much thinner back then. His shoulders were broad, his arms thick with muscle.

Suddenly, Jed came to a stop and she crashed into his broad back. His scent surrounded her. Sandalwood and leather. Manly. Sexy. She breathed him in before forcing herself to take a step back. Her entire body felt like it had been given an electric shock. A burst of adrenaline.

Like she'd eaten too much sugar and was on a high.

He turned, and grabbed hold of her. "You all right?" he asked gruffly.

"Yes. Sorry. You stopped so suddenly, it surprised me is all."

He let her go and took a step back. "Not like you not to pay attention to your surroundings."

No, it wasn't. The only time she'd ever really let down her guard was when he was around. She didn't tell him that.

"People change, I guess."

"Over ten years? Yeah, they do."

Silence fell. And it wasn't a good silence. They stood a few feet apart from each other, not saying or doing anything. In the distance, from the direction of the cookout, came the sound of laughter. The food had smelled amazing and everyone she'd met so far had been friendly.

There wasn't a friendly vibe coming from Jed.

"So, do you live here now?" she asked him, desperate to break the silence.

"Yes."

"Not in San Diego?" That was where he'd lived a few years ago.

"No."

All right then. This was like trying to pull teeth with tweezers.

"You're no longer in the Navy?"

"No."

"Did something happen and you can now only give one-word answers?" she said with exasperation.

He leaned forward slightly. "Nope."

Ouch. That stung.

"What about your wife?" she asked bravely.

"Don't have one."

She took a step back, surprised at that. What had happened?

"You were engaged."

He stiffened and she knew that she'd made a mistake. "How'd you know that?"

Shit. What could she say that didn't make her sound like a desperate stalker? "I guess I heard it somewhere."

"That so?"

Yeah. He totally didn't buy her lame answer.

"I think it would be better if I left."

"Why are you here?" he snapped.

"I'm renting a house from Ellie. In Russell. She invited me here."

He shook his head. "Too much of a coincidence. I don't like coincidences. There's gotta be a reason you're here after all this time. Is it the money, that it?"

"W-what money?"

"Fucking bullshit," he muttered.

She took in a breath, trying to calm her bubbling stomach. "I'm not sure what you're talking about, but I should go as it's obvious you're upset."

"I'm not upset. But if you came here wanting something from me, just tellin' you, you're not gonna get it."

She stared at him, unsure what to say. For the first time in years, she'd done something for herself. Moving here. Starting a new life. She was sick of being the person everyone came to, relied on, tired of making all the decisions.

And it seemed she'd made the wrong decision. Again.

"I don't want anything from you. I had no idea you lived here. Last I knew, you were living in San Diego and engaged. It's obvious that you don't want me here and so I'm going to leave. I. . .so. . .bye," she said awkwardly.

Dork.

Her dignity lasted until she got to her car. She managed to hold it together until she reached the gate.

And then she lost it.

3

Daisy snuggled under the blanket and watched Ally James, librarian and super sleuth track down the bad guy. Man, she was smart. And composed. And beautiful. She had a mom who loved her, friends, a job and an awesome hobby.

She's not real, Daisy. You're jealous of a fictional character.

She also had a hot boyfriend. Even if he did nothing more than kiss her. Sometimes Daisy thought he should be a bit more domineering, take-charge. Jed would never allow someone he loved to get into such dangerous situations. . .and she really needed to stop thinking about Jed.

She sniffled and reached into her bowl of peanut butter M&Ms, shoving a handful in her mouth. She'd thought moving here would be a new chapter for her.

She'd never expected to see Jed again

Tears welled. Fuck. She needed to do something quick to squash them.

Reese's peanut butter cups. That's what she needed. But they were in the kitchen and she was all comfy on the sofa. She paused Ally. She'd gotten her guy anyway.

Daisy sighed. "Stop being jealous, it's pathetic. Maybe you'd have a boyfriend if you actually tried going out and meeting people."

Kind of difficult to meet anyone when you were almost a total recluse. It had taken every ounce of courage she had to go to the cookout three nights ago. And she had none left. She probably wouldn't leave the house for a month.

She shuffled into the kitchen, feeling way older than her twenty-seven years and opened a cupboard, pulling out a bag of individually wrapped Reese's peanut butter cups. Yeah, she had a thing for peanut butter and chocolate. It was a match made in heaven.

Unlike her and Jed.

She groaned. "Jesus, that was cheesy."

She decided she better grab a bag of gummy bears for good measure and poured them out into another bowl. She figured if you put it all in a bowl then it counted as real food rather than candy.

Ally would put candy in a bowl rather than eating it from the packet. Ally was class.

Not trailer trash.

The pain bit deep and she had to breathe through it.

She walked back to the sofa, aware that she probably should have done more these past few days than sit and mope and stuff herself with sugar.

Tomorrow. Tomorrow, she'd pick herself back up and get on with her life. What did she care what Jed thought of her? He wasn't part of her life anymore. This was Daisy time.

She was fine on her own. Just because society seemed to dictate that she should mate and procreate, didn't mean she had to. There were plenty of single, happy people. She'd been single since she was seventeen and she was doing just fine. She looked down at her stained pajamas, the mess of candy wrappers and empty soda cans lining the coffee table.

Hmm. Maybe not fine. But she'd be okay. She always was.

She grabbed some gummy bears and scooped them into her mouth. Strawberry and orange burst on her tongue.

Delicious.

The skies opened and rain pelted the roof just as the doorbell sounded.

Shit. Who could that be? She glanced at the clock on the mantel. It was after ten. Her heart raced as she looked around for something that would serve as a weapon.

Whoever it was, she wasn't answering the door. Nope. Not happening.

JED POUNDED on the door to Ellie's place. He wouldn't think of it as Daisy's, even though she was renting it from Ellie and Bear. He ground his teeth together. He'd had to get the address from Bear, but only after he'd promised Ellie that he wouldn't be mean to Daisy.

He wasn't going to be mean to her. He wasn't an asshole. But he needed to make it clear that if she'd come here to get something from him, then she'd best just pack up and leave.

Rain pelted down. Well, maybe not tonight. It wouldn't be safe driving on the roads at night in the rain. But tomorrow, she was gone.

And even though it had been ten years and he should have put all of this behind him, her turning up had rocked him. Something he did not like.

"Daisy, I know you're in there. Let me in."

He could see the light on inside. Unless she'd changed, Daisy was a night owl. If things had been different and she'd been his, he'd have had a fight on his hands getting her poor sleeping habits under control.

Of course, a few good spankings would have helped reinforce his rules. He breathed out deep. He needed to get rid of this rage. Anger was never a productive emotion. He was always cool and calm. Always.

Except, it seemed, when it came to her.

He knocked again. "Daisy. Open up. Now."

If anyone needed some boundaries it was Daisy. She'd never had that from her parents. Her mom wasn't even sure which one of her clients was her dad. He'd certainly not stuck around, and that was even if he knew he had a kid.

Her mother had mostly been drunk or high. From a young age Daisy had to look out for herself. And then once her siblings came along, she'd taken care of them as well. He wondered where Bradley and Sylvie were. They'd be what, twenty-three and twenty now? Something like that.

"Daisy!" Bang. Bang. Bang.

The door suddenly opened and he stood there, frozen with his fist in the air. She stared up at him, her gray eyes wide and frightened, her face pale, her worn pajamas stained and crinkled. Her short hair stood up in tufts as though she'd been pulling at it or running her fingers through it over and over.

She had a smudge of something in the corner of her lips and he had to fight the ridiculous urge to lean forward and lick it off.

Not here for that.

"What are you doing here?" she asked.

"Came to talk to you. Did you check to see who it was before you opened the door?"

She frowned, staring up at him incredulously. "You were yelling loud enough to wake the whole neighborhood. I knew who it was."

Oh. Right.

"You should still check," he grumbled, unable to let that pass, even as he told himself it wasn't his place to lecture her. "And why did it take you so long to answer the door?"

"Umm, maybe because you were yelling loud enough to wake the neighborhood?" she replied sarcastically. "What do you want? I'm about to go to bed."

"No, you're not. You never go to bed before midnight."

"Well, maybe I'm a different person than I was before. Maybe I go to bed early these days."

He just looked at her disbelievingly.

"Why are you here, bashing my door down in the middle of a storm?"

He sighed. "First, this is just a bit of rain, not a storm. Second, if I wanted to bash your door in, then I would have. I'm coming in."

He stepped forward but she didn't shift out of the way, which honestly shocked him. He wasn't used to not getting his way. He intimidated most people. And the way she'd reacted to him the other night, leaving without barely a word of protest, he'd figured she wouldn't give him any trouble.

"No, you're not," she said stubbornly.

"It's raining out here," he pointed out.

"I can see that."

"You want to have this conversation with me on your doorstep, standing in the rain?"

"You're under a porch so technically the rain isn't getting on you. And I don't want to have any conversation with you."

He ground his teeth together. *Patience. Patience.*

"Get out of the way, Daisy."

"No."

"You owe me a few minutes of your time, don't you think?" He was seconds away from picking her up and moving her.

She just stared at him then she let out a long sigh that had him longing to bend her over his knee, but finally she stepped back and flung out a hand. "Be my guest."

"Thank you," he replied, stomping inside.

"Figured you weren't going to leave until you had your say and I don't want the neighbors calling the cops."

"Worried about me going to jail?"

"Don't have time for the paperwork," she replied quickly.

He shouldn't find her amusing. Only this was the Daisy he remembered. The one with too much sass and spit for her own good, as his grandfather would say.

He took off his jacket and hung it on a hook then sitting on the bench in the foyer, removed his boots.

"Make yourself at home," she said sarcastically. She turned away, heading into the living room. He followed then came to a stop, looking around. There was a huge, soft pale pink blanket on the sofa, which she'd obviously been cuddled up in. Big throw pillows occupied most of the couch. Fairy lights had been strung across the mantel. She'd always loved fairy lights.

"See you've made yourself at home."

"This is my home," she shot back.

He took in the mess of wrappers and bowls filled with candy and chocolate.

"Looks like Willy Wonka threw up in here."

"That's ridiculous," she said snootily, but she did start picking up empty cans of pop and candy wrappers.

"How much sugar have you had today?"

"Not nearly enough for this," she muttered. She sent him a withering look before disappearing into the kitchen. He glanced around the rest of the house. It was huge. He wondered why she'd rented such a big place. . .unless. . .

"Do you have kids?" he asked as she returned. Bear and Ellie hadn't said anything. But it would explain the big house and the excess of candy. Although, who would let their kids eat this much crap?

"No."

"Strange."

"What? Why?" She gave him a puzzled look.

"Just figured Bobby-John would have knocked you up. From what I hear he thought condoms were the devil's work."

She made a funny face. What? She didn't like to be reminded of her time with Bobby-John?

"He marry you?"

He told himself he didn't care about her answer, but his hands were clenched into fists. To hide the telling sign, he strode to one of the overstuffed armchairs and sat. She remained standing, just staring down at him. If she thought the higher position gave her more power, she was sadly mistaken.

"No, he didn't, uh, marry me." She sounded off. He could always tell when she was lying, her nose tended to twitch and her voice grew higher. This wasn't a lie, but it was something else. It was obvious she didn't want to talk about Bobby-John.

"There. . .there's something you need to know about Bobby-John. He—"

"Daisy, I'm not here to talk about Bobby-John," he interrupted, even though he'd been the one to bring up BJ.

"Then why are you here?" she whispered.

"Here to tell you that if you're here 'cause of the money, then you are way off base thinking I have any feelings for you left. I don't."

As he spoke, her face grew confused.

"You said something about money the other night, but I still have no idea what you're talking about."

He leaned forward, resting his forearms on his thighs. He clasped his hands together, dropping them between his legs.

"You know my grandfather died eight months ago?"

A strange look crossed her face. "Yes."

At least she was that honest.

"Sorry for your loss," she muttered.

He nodded. "I inherited everything from him."

She stared at him for a moment then her eyes widened. "And you. . .you really think that I'm here because I want that money?"

"Can't think of any other reason you would be."

"You really think that little of me?"

"Don't have reason to think any better of you."

The pain that filled her face nearly had him softening. But he couldn't do that. He needed to make this clear.

What if you're wrong? What if her being here is just a coincidence?

Didn't matter. He still didn't want her here.

"I did not come here for you," she told him in a low voice. "I'm here for me. A fresh start. I certainly am not here for any money. I wouldn't take a cent of that man's money even if I was starving and living on the streets!"

SHE GLARED DOWN AT HIM. She felt ill over the idea that he thought she could be here for that old bastard's money. Never. It hurt that he could think that badly of her, but she guessed she couldn't blame him. He didn't know the truth of what had happened.

Not that it seemed he was interested in learning.

Her phone started ringing and she picked it up, looked at the screen.

"Leave it," he grumbled.

She ignored him and answered the call. A hint of dread filled her stomach, tightening it into knots. Sylvie never called unless she wanted something. And Daisy's well was starting to run dry. "Sylvie, sweetie? Everything okay?"

A sob greeted her on the other end.

"Sylvie? What's wrong? What's going on?"

"All men are bastards."

The knot in her stomach unraveled. So it was a problem with Jack, Sylvie's boyfriend. Personally, she didn't like him but she'd always been careful not to say anything to Sylvie. Her sister had a fiery temper to match her red hair and Daisy knew that a surefire way to get on her sister's bad side was to say something about her jerk boyfriend.

Unfortunately, that meant Sylvie often got hurt, since she seemed to have a knack for choosing the worst men.

"Oh sweetheart, what happened?" She didn't say anything about the fact that she hadn't heard from Sylvie in days, since she'd left Kansas City to drive here. That she hadn't answered Daisy's multiple texts and had let her calls go to voicemail.

Nope. She didn't say anything about that right now. Sylvie was hurting. She didn't need her sister getting on her case.

"He-he's been cheating on me!"

"Please stop crying. Are you all right? Where are you?" Music thumped through the phone. Was she at a club? Shoot. And Daisy couldn't get to her to pick her up. Guilt filled her.

"Sylvie, please talk to me. Have you been drinking? Do you have a ride home?"

More sobs. Shit. What was she going to do? Then suddenly the phone was plucked from her hand. "Hey, what the hell do you think you're doing?"

WHAT WAS HE DOING? He wasn't sure. He only knew he'd had enough of sitting here, being ignored, listening to her grow more agitated and worried.

"Sylvie? Are you there?" he barked.

At once the sobs he'd heard stopped. That happened awfully quickly.

"Who is this?" she asked. He stepped back from Daisy, who was trying to snatch the phone from his hand.

"One moment and I will explain." He placed his hand over the mouthpiece, ignoring the outraged spluttering on the other end. It seemed he would have to deal with one female at a time.

"Daisy, sit down," he said firmly.

"Give me my damn phone back. You have no right to take it. That's my sister on the other end. Give it to me."

He just pointed at the sofa and shook his head. She stomped her foot. Brat. "Sit. Now. You tried to figure out what's happened, she obviously wasn't answering you. It's my turn."

"She doesn't even know you!"

"Do you want to stand here debating the point, with your sister growing more agitated or are you going to behave yourself and sit?"

She saluted him.

Total brat.

But she sat. A sense of satisfaction went through him.

"Sylvie, are you there?"

"Yes, who are you? Where's my sister? Is she all right?"

"Your sister is fine. Now that she's behaving herself."

Daisy gasped and gave him an outraged look. She attempted to stand; he shot her a stern look and she sat back down. Good.

"Sylvie, I'm Jed Carson. You probably don't remember me—"

"I know who you are. What are *you* doing there?"

He ignored that question. "What seems to be the problem?"

There was another beat of silence. He could hear music in the background. She was calling her sister from a bar?

"Do you need a ride home? Have you called a taxi?"

"I can get myself home," she muttered. "I want to talk to my sister."

"No," he replied. He knew he was being high-handed and an

asshole. But if the sister was in actual danger, then Daisy wasn't equipped to handle the situation.

"Sylvie? Tell me what is going on? Where are you?"

"My asshole boyfriend is a cheating bastard."

He raised his eyebrows. Right. "Sorry to hear that. That's the only reason you wish to speak to your sister?" He had no experience with cheating boyfriends. Obviously.

"Yes. No. I need some money. I'm broke. I haven't got enough cash to pay for a taxi home."

"Right. I see." He put his hand back over the mouthpiece. "Your sister needs money for a taxi home."

Daisy frowned. "But I just sent her some two days ago. It's all gone?"

He didn't like the sound of that. She was still supporting her siblings? "Is she in college? Does she not work?"

She shook her head. "No, she works full-time. I just send money to help out. Tell her I'm putting some into her account right now."

"Your sister is putting taxi money into your account," he told Sylvie. Not his business.

"Okay. Good. Thanks. Can you tell her I'll call her tomorrow?" She'd hung up the phone before he could even reply. Hmm. Seemed she'd called less to complain about the asshole boyfriend and more because she needed money. He was starting not to like Daisy's sister much.

Daisy rushed back into the room. "Done. Can I talk to her now?" She held out her hand, her exasperation clear.

He felt bad about having to tell her Sylvie had ended the call as soon as she'd heard her sister was transferring the funds.

"We got cut off," he told her. "Think she said something about her phone going dead."

"Oh. Well. I'm glad she got time to tell you what she needed. Of course, if you hadn't stolen my phone, I could have figured out what was going on quicker and had time to find out what happened with Jack-the-jerk."

She glared up at him. He wondered why the hell he'd felt the need to guard her feelings. Why did he care? He damn well shouldn't.

He needed to get out of here. Away from her.

"I'm going. Listen, do us both a favor. Leave town. I'll talk to Ellie about releasing you from the lease." He couldn't have her here. He couldn't be at Sanctuary knowing that she was just an hour's drive away. He delivered the final blow. "There's nothing for you here. And there never will be."

THE NEXT MORNING, she sat cuddled up on the sofa. A blanket settled around her like a hug. Normally being snuggled up brought her a lot of comfort. But not right then. She was still reeling from what happened last night.

There's nothing for you here.

Yeah, she was getting that. She didn't need to be smacked around the face with it to make her see it.

Didn't she? Only a fool would have come here, chasing a man after ten years. A man who didn't want her.

Do us both a favor.

Her thumb crept its way into her mouth as she shuffled the worn piece of material back and forth beneath her nose, inhaling the scent. It was actually just part of a blanket she'd had since she was a child. It had gradually worn away until only a rough square was left.

She knew it was kind of ridiculous that at her age she still had a snuggly and that she liked to suck her thumb. Nobody else knew about it. Wasn't like she ever shared her bed with anyone. And her siblings certainly didn't know. She'd always kept it in a special box under the bed, bringing it out only when she needed it.

Which was pretty much every night.

She sighed. She really needed to get up. After Jed left, well more like stormed out of the house last night, she'd gorged herself on a whole block of chocolate, felt so ill and upset that she'd vomited most of that back up and then she'd climbed into bed, only to spend most of the night tossing and turning.

Now she had a killer headache and her stomach still felt miserable. She'd never been much of a drinker so she could only guess that this is what a hangover felt like. Still, she had clients with deadlines and she didn't have the right to wallow in misery and let them down. That would be a surefire way to lose them.

So, she took a deep breath and pushed all the hurt from last night down deep. Deep inside where no one would get it and she slammed the lid on that box shut and locked it. She was certain at a later date, that it would come back to haunt her. But right now, she needed to function.

The phone rang and she groaned. Who would be calling her? Sylvie? She quickly pushed off the blanket and rolled, grabbing it and answering the call without even bothering to look at the caller ID.

"Hello? Sylvie, is that you?"

"Um, no, sorry, it's Ellie."

Ellie? Oh shit, Ellie. Her landlady. Well, soon to be ex-landlady she guessed. Sadness filled her.

"Oh, right, sorry, Ellie."

"Is now a good time to talk?"

"Sure. I guess so." She sat up, having to bite back a whimper of pain as knives slashed through her head.

"You all right?" Ellie asked, sounding concerned. "You sound like you're in pain."

Tears welled in her eyes at the other woman's concern.

"Sugar hangover," she told her. "I ate my weight in chocolate last night. And gummy bears. And I think there were even a few Twizzlers."

There was a beat of silence. Then Ellie burst into laughter. "Oh sorry, I shouldn't laugh. I can't say as I've ever had a sugar hangover. I don't think I've ever eaten that much chocolate before though."

"Stick with me, I'll show you how. Sugar is my crack."

More giggles. Then they died off. "A sugar hangover the next day doesn't sound that pleasant."

It wasn't. It really wasn't.

"I hear you're leaving." There was a note of sadness to Ellie's voice that cut her to the quick.

"You've spoken to Jed."

"Yeah. I get that you two have history, but you don't have to go, do you?"

Now she felt terrible.

Worthless slut.

Her breath left her in a shuddering gasp and she reached down to pinch her thigh. Hard. So hard tears entered her eyes.

She was not worthless. Or a slut.

"I don't want to leave," she whispered, surprising herself. Surprising Ellie too if the silence that filled the phone was anything to go by.

There was nothing for her back in Kansas City. Sylvie didn't need her. Except for money. She sucked in a breath. She knew deep down that that's the reason why she'd called last night. Not because she was upset about Jack-the-jerk. If she needed someone to talk to then she'd call her friends.

Not her sister.

After all, what did Daisy know about men?

Not a thing.

Do us both a favor.

Why did she have to leave town? She loved this house. She'd only been here a week, but she'd made a place for herself. And she barely went anywhere so what were the odds she would run into him?

"You don't want to leave? But I thought Jed said. . ."

"I know he's your friend and—"

"Actually, I don't know him that well," Ellie interrupted. "Bear knows him a bit better than me, but I'm not sure anyone knows Jed that well. I mean, we're loyal to him, he's a part of Sanctuary so if you hurt him, I will come after you."

The threat might have made her laugh under other circumstances, Ellie was tiny and she didn't appear to have a mean bone in her body, but it just made her feel sad. Because she didn't have that sort of loyalty, not even from her own family.

They love me. They're just independent. Adventurous.

Uh-huh.

"I understand. I'll pack up and be out of here by the end of the day." Turns out it was a good thing her belongings fit into the trunk of her car.

"No, that's not what I mean," Ellie said. "I know that I don't know you either, but I like you, Daisy. And you seem a bit sad and lost. I don't want you to leave. Sounds like you don't want that either."

"I'm just. . .tired."

"Yeah, I get that. When I crashed during that snow storm, I was exhausted from taking care of my parents for years. They were sick. Or at least they made me think they were sick. I did everything for them and I was just tired. Then I met Bear. And he showed me that there are people out there who are good. Kind. Honest. Now we look out for each other."

"I want that." Shit. Did she just say that? "Damn, I think that chocolate last night had something in it that loosened my tongue."

Ellie giggled again. "Look, why don't you stay awhile? See if you like it here?"

"Jed doesn't want me here."

"Jed ain't God."

She let out a startled laugh.

"Look, I might be loyal to him because he's one of us, but that doesn't mean I can't be loyal to you too. Just don't hurt him and we're good, all right?"

"I didn't know Jed lived here. Honestly. This is some weird coincidence. Saw this house online and felt like it was where I was meant to be."

"I get that," Ellie said quietly. "Don't go. Jed probably won't even notice you're still here."

She sucked in a breath at that. Ouch.

"I didn't mean that the way it sounded," Ellie said quickly. "Oh shit. I just meant that he hardly ever leaves the ranch except for work. That's all."

"It's okay," she said quietly. "You're right. He won't notice." And even if he did, well, she'd just have to make it clear that she hadn't stayed because of him.

She just had to figure out how to do that.

"I'll stay."

The squeal that hit her ears made her flinch and then grin. Well, at least someone was happy she was here.

4

"I've decided to try online dating," Daisy told Ellie as soon as she picked up the phone. She was sitting in front of her laptop, staring at the dating website in front of her, her stomach rolling with nerves. She felt so ill she thought she might vomit. Even the big bowl of ice cream with Hershey's chocolate sauce poured over the top wasn't tempting her. In fact, she'd barely managed to eat or sleep these past few days.

Since Jed told her to leave.

Part of her worried that he would turn up again, demanding to know why she hadn't done what he'd ordered. The other part of her was disappointed that he hadn't arrived on her doorstep, demanding to know why she hadn't done what he'd ordered.

Contrary much?

When he'd looked at her so coldly a part of her shriveled up and died. She didn't like that she was so vulnerable to him. She thought she'd built up walls to protect herself. Turns out that didn't work against Jed. She hadn't made them Jed-proof.

Damn it.

"Shut up," Ellie said.

"What?" she asked distractedly. What sort of photo did she have that she could upload? Did she even have a current one?

"You are not online dating."

"I am." Well, thinking about it. "How else am I going to meet someone?"

"You don't need a dating site. I know heaps of handsome single guys just looking for a special relationship with a girl like you."

What did that mean? "A girl like me? What single and desperate? An introvert with no life?"

"You have a life. Although when is the last time you left the house?"

Umm.

"The cookout?" she guessed. Online shopping made it so much easier to stay in the house and hide.

Ellie sighed. "Maybe you would meet someone if you got out and about. What if the guy you go out with is some sort of psycho axe murderer?"

"I don't think there's a category for that on Tinder."

"Smart-ass."

"Don't worry. I'm sure there are better ways for axe murderers to find victims."

Ellie sighed. "I worry about you."

"I'm fine. I just. . .I don't want to regret not trying. I'm not ready to end up a lonely old maid. And my idea to meet a guy by hanging out in the meat aisle of the grocery store doesn't seem to be working," she joked.

"You eat meat? I thought you lived on candy and chocolate."

"Pretty much, guys 'round here don't look like they eat much sugar though." Most of the men she'd seen were fit and ripped.

"I don't think any of JSI's boys do," Ellie replied. "Their bodies are their temples. And boy, you can tell."

"Says the woman with her own hunk of spunk." Whoops. What if Ellie took offense to her noticing how gorgeous her man was?

But Ellie just sighed dreamily. "He sure is."

Daisy made pretend gagging noises.

"Oh hush," Ellie told her. "You won't be a lonely old maid. Let me set you up."

"With who?" she asked suspiciously.

"There's a number of really great guys here at Sanctuary," Ellie said enthusiastically.

"That's not a good idea."

"Why not?"

"Because Jed lives there? What if they're friends with him? What if we fall in love and I move in with them? How awkward would that be?"

"Daisy, what you and Jed had was over a long time ago." She'd told Ellie the very basics of how they knew each other.

"Ouch," she muttered.

"Not saying it to be mean, but I'm sure he wouldn't worry if you started dating a guy from here."

She wasn't so sure. Ellie hadn't seen the way that Jed had looked at her.

"I'm gonna try the online dating thing, if it doesn't work out, I'll let you fix me up. Deal?"

There was silence. "You tell me when you're going out and where and with who and you text me when you leave and when you get home."

"Yes, Mom," she said teasingly although it filled her with warmth to have someone worry about her. "It will be fine. I might meet Prince Charming."

Ellie snorted. "You're more likely to meet Jack the Ripper."

"Thanks, that makes me feel so much better."

"What friends are for," Ellie said cheerfully.

Hopefully this would be the start of something. She could have something for herself. A new start.

Yeah, she liked the idea of that.

HE'D BEEN A JERK.

These last few days, he'd done a lot of thinking and that was the conclusion he'd come to. He'd been taken by surprise, probably overreacted and he'd had no right to tell her to leave town. He'd wanted to think the worst of her. He hadn't wanted to look at her and see vulnerability. To see her sweetness. To see hurt in her eyes.

Hurt that he caused.

Yep. Class A jerk.

Her searching him out now because of his inheritance made little sense. Plus, she'd seemed genuinely angry when he'd accused her of being after the money. Christ, that damn money was a headache. He had no idea what to do with what his grandfather left him. He didn't need that sort of cash. So he'd just been sitting on it.

He hadn't expected the sight of her to hit him so hard. For there to be this sharp stab of longing. Of arousal. Of need.

His phone rang as he entered his cabin and he took the call even though it was the last thing he felt like doing. He'd just gotten home. He was exhausted. He wanted to shower, eat and sleep. Maybe not in that order.

"Jed. It's Bear."

"What's up?" Jed asked, moving into his cabin and dumping his bag on the floor.

"It's Daisy."

"Daisy? Is everything all right? Has she left?"

It's for the best.

"No, she hasn't. Ellie convinced her to stay."

Something filled him, something that felt like relief.

"Bear?" he prompted when the other man said nothing more. "Is Daisy all right?"

"Ellie just told me she's gone on a date tonight. With some guy she met. Online." Bear sounded horrified and disgusted.

A knot formed in his gut. "She fucking did not!"

"She did, man. Was going to go track her down myself, but thought I'd see where your head was at."

"Where my head is at?"

"I don't know everything that happened between you two. Daisy has told Ellie some of it. I do know that you don't react the way you did to someone you feel nothing about."

"Does Ellie know where they've gone?" he asked, not about to go there with Bear.

"Yep."

"Well?"

"Not giving that to you until you tell me where your head is at," Bear replied calmly. "I came to you out of courtesy, in case you still have feelings for her. But if you're just going after her because you want to tell her to leave town again then I'm going to go myself."

"I'm not going to tell her to leave town," Jed bit out. He wasn't going into any more detail. But Bear seemed to get it.

"Thought it might be like that. Go gentle man, a lot of things can happen in ten years."

Like he didn't know that. His jaw tightened as he got the name of the bar where she was meeting this guy. That it was one of the roughest bars in the state didn't help his temper. He ended the call with Bear, put his boots back on, then his jacket, and slammed the door on his way out.

He wasn't quite sure what he was going to do when he found Daisy. All he knew was that there would be no more blind dates.

And that he wasn't as done with her as he'd thought.

THE DATE SUCKED.

Boy, did it suck. She'd only been on the dating site for a few hours when she'd received a request for a date. The guy had sounded good. His name was Mike Lyle. He worked in IT, mostly from home. Seemed polite, nice-looking, and he wanted to go out for dinner.

She'd said yes.

What had she been thinking? Why hadn't she listened to Ellie? Mike was supposed to be thirty-four, but he looked about fifty. Not that she was worried about his looks. But he was so bland and boring it was all she could do not to go into a coma. He talked. A lot. About himself. And his two ex-wives, who apparently had taken him to the cleaners.

Because that's something she wanted to hear about.

Pretty much the first thing he'd said to her was that she had to pay for her own meal and drink. She hadn't been intending to let him pay, but it still put the date off to a weird start.

They were halfway through the first course and he hadn't noticed that she wasn't talking. Not that she could get a word in anyway. She pushed her plate away even though it was still mostly full. How long until Ellie called? She was supposed to call half way through the date and see if Daisy needed an excuse to leave.

She really needed an excuse to leave.

"And do you know how much fucking lawyers cost nowadays? Should have fucking trained to be a lawyer, that's what I should have done. Are you gonna eat that?"

She looked down at the steak she'd only taken a few bites of and before she'd finished shaking her head, he'd whipped it off her plate.

"Can't let it go to waste. This is fucking good steak. That's why I brought you here. Best fucking steak in the state."

Seriously? This place was a dive. The lighting was dim, which she figured was a good thing as it no doubt hid a variety of sins. And it stunk of stale beer and cigarette smoke.

She needed to get out of here.

"I think this date is going great, don't you? Wanna make a time for a second date?"

What? So, he could eat her steak and make her pay? And complain about his ex-wives all night? And chew with his mouth open so she could see everything?

"It's refreshing not to have a woman chatter on all the time, you know? Nag, nag, nag, was all I ever got from my bitch ex-wives."

"Maybe if you had refrained from calling them bitches and swearing at them constantly, they would have stuck around. And you could have tried listening to what they had to say instead of complaining about them nagging at you."

The deep voice sent a shiver of goosebumps up her back. He wasn't here. He couldn't be here. He wasn't. Seriously, that was someone else standing behind her, talking in that deep rumble that made her insides dance with happiness and her body clench with need.

Mike glared up at the stranger standing behind her who was, for some odd reason, interrupting their date to tell Mike what a jerk he was.

Thanks, kind stranger.

"Excuse me?"

"You heard me," the stranger replied. She was not turning around to look at him. She was not.

Mike opened his mouth, closed it. "What the hell? You got no right to interrupt our date and talk to me like that, you fucking asshole." Mike looked at her. "Do you know this fucking dickhead?"

She shook her head. Then a hand landed on her shoulder. Its heat seeped through her clothing as though it wasn't even there, searing the skin beneath. Branding it.

Okay, now you're just getting fanciful. He's just touching you.

"Daisy's leaving with me now," the stranger who somehow knew her name said. "She won't be going on any more dates with you. Do not contact her."

"Now see here," Mike started to say, standing. "You cannot just steal my date!"

"I can when she was mine first."

Fuck. Fuckity fuck.

She turned to look up at Jed. Big mistake. His jaw was tight with tension. He didn't shift his gaze away from Mike, but she could tell his glare was intense. Fury rolled off him in frightening waves.

Shit. Why hadn't Ellie called?

"What's he talking about?" Mike asked. "You fucking seeing him too? Well, this is my turn with her tonight, buddy, so wait for yours."

"You are not having a turn with her. She's not some toy. Come, Daisy. Now."

All right, that was not a voice you disobeyed and she found herself rising. She tried to find some anger for his high-handedness. But truth was, she was grateful for anything that meant she didn't have to listen to Mike moan for another hour. She reached for her bag to grab out her wallet.

"I'm sorry about this," she said to Mike. "Let me get some cash to cover my dinner."

"Why? Seems he ate it all," Jed bit off.

She fumbled with her wallet then watched in amazement as Jed dropped a fifty-dollar bill on the table. "That should cover it."

She'd say. The steak only cost $12.95, which she was betting was the real reason Moany Mike had brought her here. Best steak in the state her ass.

Jed wrapped his arm around her waist and pulled her with him.

She tried to turn back to say good night, but he tightened his grip around her waist. "Do not even think about it."

"You're being super rude." She glared up at him.

"No, being rude would have been just picking you up and carrying you out of here over my shoulder. That's still an option if you don't behave yourself."

"Behave myself?" she gasped. "I'm not a child."

Jed snorted. "Sure act like one at times."

"I do not." She was highly insulted by that. She'd raised both of her siblings. She'd always been the adult. She had never had a chance to be a child.

"You're impulsive, you do things without thinking them through like going on dates with strangers."

"I used an online dating app; people use them all the time!"

By this time, they were in the small foyer of the restaurant. He grabbed her jacket off the rack then he held it out for her to slip her arms in. That was surprisingly gentlemanly.

"What?" he asked, staring down at her with one eyebrow raised. "You didn't think I'd have manners?"

"No, it's not that." Of course, he would. He'd always opened doors for her, always walked on the outside of the footpath, said his grandfather taught him how to treat a lady. "People change."

He nodded. "They do. Just what did you think you were doing going on a blind date? Why would you meet someone here? This place is dodgy as hell, did you do no research first?"

She hadn't. But she wasn't going to tell him that "It's a public space. I doubt anything bad would happen to me here."

"It's a biker bar and someone was murdered in the parking lot six months ago."

She gaped up at him, so shocked that she let him take her hand without protest. He led her outside. "They were not."

"They were. And you just met some stranger here."

"Mike isn't a murderer."

"Maybe not. But he is an asshole. What kind of jerk talks about his ex-wives and makes his date pay for her meal?" The disgust in his voice nearly made her smile.

But she didn't want him thinking that she was a total fool. "I'm not an idiot. Ellie knew where I was. She was supposed to call me at nine to give me an out if I needed it. I better call her and make sure she's all right."

"Ellie is fine. What Ellie is not, is suitable back-up. You're just lucky Bear discovered what was going on and called me. What would Ellie have done if he'd turned out to be a rapist or murderer, huh?"

"Do you have an unusually high number of murderers in Montana?" she asked with exasperation.

He came to a stop beside a huge-ass, black truck and turned to look down at her.

"What kind of question is that?"

"It's just you all seem to have this crazy idea that murderers use dating sites to pick their next victims."

"Doesn't seem so crazy to me." He beeped open the truck. Figured. It matched its owner's personality. Dark and stormy.

He opened the passenger door lifted her and placed her in the seat.

"Hey! What are you doing?"

"I'm taking you home."

"I have my car here."

"Well, at least you didn't let him pick you up. Please tell me he doesn't know where you live."

"Of course, he doesn't!"

He reached over her to do up her seatbelt. She slapped his hand then she froze and stared down at him without breathing. He leaned back and watched her. The interior light of the truck was on, and at least he didn't look mad. Or stern. In fact, there was concern on his face. "Daisy, you scared of me?"

"N-no."

He narrowed his gaze. "Don't want you to be scared of me. But I also want you to know that I won't take you lying to me. Gonna ask you again, you think I'll hurt you?"

"Not physically," she muttered.

"You had a guy who's hurt you in the past?" There was a stillness about him that made her wary.

"No."

He breathed out a sigh. Then he gently cupped her face with his palm. "I won't ever hit you. Won't hurt you. Definitely gonna spank you. No doubt you'll be over my knee in the future, but that's all about me keeping you safe and you knowing that if you cross boundaries and break rules that there are consequences."

She just stared at him; aware her mouth had dropped open. What the hell was going on? Was she dreaming? Being pranked?

He placed a finger under her chin, lifting it so her mouth closed. "Gonna catch flies like that. Now settle in. I'm taking you home. I'll arrange to have your car dropped off to you in the morning, okay?"

She didn't say anything. Couldn't say anything. And he backed away and shut the door.

She should use this opportunity to get away. Obviously, he had lost his mind. What was he even doing here? So he'd found out from Bear that she was on a date but what did he care? He didn't want anything to do with her. He'd made that clear. And yet here he was, telling Moany Mike that he was a dick, paying for her meal —which she fully intended to pay him back for, helping her into her coat, driving her home. . .

Threatening to spank her.

What was with that? He wouldn't hurt her but he would spank her if she broke some rules, of which she knew nothing about?

"I've entered an alternate reality," she muttered.

She jumped as she heard a chuckle and she turned to stare at him where he sat in the driver's seat.

"You feeling all right?"

"Are you?" she countered.

He belted up. "Yeah, I'm feeling great." He looked her up and down. "For the first time in a long time, everything feels right."

And what the hell was she supposed to do with that?

JED FLICKED his gaze over to his silent passenger. Funny, he'd expected her to be angry. Upset. He hadn't expected silent. She'd always been a bit reserved. Aloof. But with other people. Never him.

Because she trusted him.

Had. She had trusted him. They no longer had trust between them and her shields were fully up.

What if Bear hadn't found out about this date? What if she'd gone on other dates? With guys worse than that prick he'd just found her with? She had no business dating other guys when he. . .

When he what? He took a deep breath. He'd come to the conclusion as he was breaking the speed limit to get to her, his gut tied in a knot the entire time, that he was only going to find some peace was by exploring whatever it was that obviously still existed between them. These feelings that had been stirred to life by her return.

But he got that she was confused. So was he. He'd come on strong. He'd interrupted her date, pulled her out of there and basically told her that she needed rules and discipline. And she. . .

Hadn't hit him. Or told him he was a jerk. Hmm that was interesting. Did she want what he could give her? Boundaries and consequences?

"Guess you're wondering why I haven't left town?" she asked. "Is that why you came tonight to find me? To tell me to leave again? Are you driving me home so you can make sure I pack?"

He frowned. Fuck. He couldn't blame her for thinking that way, though. He had been a jerk the other night. He hadn't handled things well.

He didn't want to want her. He didn't want to spend these last few nights tossing and turning, thinking about her, remembering the look on her face after he'd told her to go.

This time he was going in with his eyes wide open and some rules firmly in place. He definitely had no intention of trusting her.

"I came tonight because I heard you were going on a date with a complete stranger to a bar that doesn't have the best reputation."

"You were worried about me?" There was surprise in her voice.

"Yes."

"Why?"

He took in a deep breath. "Daisy, I owe you an apology for the way I reacted at the cookout, but mostly for what I said to you the other night at your place. I had no right to tell you to leave town. You showing up out of the blue took me by surprise. I jumped to some conclusions and I didn't react well."

"You thought I searched you out for your money."

He nodded. "I did."

"I didn't. I had no idea you lived here. I'm not after anything like that," she whispered. "I hurt you. Ten years ago. When I left—"

"That was ten years ago. We were both kids and I've got no right to hold onto old shit to punish you with now. The past needs to stay there. So I'm sorry for what I said and the way I reacted. Forgive me?"

"Yes," she whispered.

"Yes?" He gave her a look of surprise. He hadn't expected it to be that easy.

"I get that you were surprised and it wasn't really a good surprise. So yes."

"Thank you," he said gruffly. "I appreciate that. I also need to hear that you won't be going on any more blind dates with strangers."

"Because you worry about me?"

"It's dangerous, Daisy. There are too many predators out there, just dying to take a bite out of you."

"Not certain I'm really that tasty."

He was.

"Got to admit, tonight's dinner didn't exactly go as I'd hoped it might."

"That guy was a dick," he stated.

"He sure did moan a lot about his ex-wives. And he talked with his mouth full. Food kept falling out and onto his lap."

"At least he was just a douche and not a murderer."

"People around here sure do have an obsession with murderers," she muttered. "It's making me rethink my plan to stay."

Well, that no longer suited him. "You want to go out for dinner, I'll take you," he offered gruffly.

There was silence. Was she horrified by the idea?

"We've never gone out for dinner before."

They hadn't? No, he realized. They had been kids. Taking her out for a meal hadn't entered his head. They'd been to the movies a few times, but he'd known it always made her feel awkward that he had to pay for everything so mostly he'd take her for a drive somewhere and they'd spend their time making out and talking.

How they'd never had sex he didn't know. Wasn't like his horny teenage self hadn't wanted to. But he'd also wanted to do right by her. She'd been special. He'd adored her, loved her...

Until the day he'd discovered she'd taken off with the biggest asshole in the county.

He pulled up outside her house and turned off the truck before hopping out and coming around to her door. She grew tense as he grabbed her around the waist and lifted her down. He deliberately brushed her body against his and felt her tremble.

"I don't. . .I still don't exactly understand what's happening here," she whispered.

"What's happening is that I had some time to think. During that time, I realized I acted hastily, said things I shouldn't. When I heard you were out on a date with another man. Someone you didn't know, I figured that the reason for my reaction is because you stirred feelings I thought had died ten years ago. I don't want you dating anyone else. I want you with me."

"You. . .you want me? So you no longer hate me?"

"Never hated you, babe. Not that." He cupped her face between his large hands. "Was mad at you. Mad at you for a long time."

"I wish you'd let me—"

"No, you don't need to tell me because it doesn't matter. From now on, we're moving forward not back, understand me? No more talk of the past, yeah?"

He waited for her nod. "Good girl. What matters is here and now." He leaned in and finally, he kissed her. He made his touch light for a start. Just a gentle brush of his mouth against hers. Then he pressed deeper, he reached around her and grabbed hold of her ass with one hand, squeezing. She opened her mouth on a gasp and he took total advantage, deepening the kiss.

His heart pounded; arousal rushed through his body.

Calm things down. Chill.

He forced himself to pull back. Last thing he wanted was to scare her off. He didn't know how much experience she had. When her last relationship had been. And his needs were intense.

He took a half-step back, holding onto her waist as she swayed slightly.

5

She looked up at him in complete shock. She really had entered an alternate universe. Because there was no way that was real. Jed Carson had not just kissed her.

Nope. Nuh-uh. Didn't happen.

Yeah? Then how come your lips are tingling? How come your clit is throbbing? Your nipples are hard? And why have you got the taste of him in your mouth?

And oh, why did it all feel so damn good?

Shit. She was so confused.

"I'm so confused."

"I know. My fault." He cupped her face between his hands. She peered up at him, even though she couldn't make out his features in the dark. "I want you to listen to me. I was wrong to tell you to go. Repeat after me. I want you to stay."

"You want me to stay." Her lips still tingled.

"You're going to stop going on blind dates."

"No more blind dates," she said obediently.

"Because you're going to be too busy with me."

Her heart raced. Busy with him.

"Come on, let's get you inside and warm. It's far too late for you to be out." He gently directed her up the porch to her front door. "Give me your key."

She dug her keys out of her handbag and handed them over without a word.

He unlocked the door and walked inside first. She followed him in and then she shut the door and locked it behind her. When she turned around, he gave her a nod of approval. "Good girl. Make sure that's always locked."

"I know," she said. "I've lived in the city a long time. I always keep it locked."

He frowned slightly for some reason. "What's wrong?" she asked.

He shook his head. "Don't mind me. Just don't like the idea of you living in some city, unprotected."

"Sylvie lived with me up until a year ago." And the relief she'd felt when her sister moved out still made her feel guilty.

"And what about Bobby?" He waved his hand before she could answer, the look in his eyes dark and dangerous. "No, don't mind. I don't want to hear about him. Other than your assurance he's out of your life."

"He better never get near me again," she whispered. She didn't know what she would do if he did. But she'd do something.

Jed eyed her for a moment then he looked like he was going to say something before he shook his head. "Where is your brother?"

"Backpacking around South America."

"Really?"

"I worry about him," she whispered. "I get scared that he'll get himself into trouble and I won't be there to help him."

He reached out and rubbed the frown line off her forehead. "He's a man now, babe. He doesn't need his big sister riding to his rescue, no matter that she's done it all his life. He needs to stand on his own two feet."

"I know," she whispered. Didn't mean she had to like it.

"You were more of a mom to those two than your own ever was."

"Hard to be a mom when you're stoned or drunk most of your life," she said bitterly.

Whoops. She glanced up at him, to find only sympathy and understanding in his eyes. "I'm real proud of you for the way you looked out for them."

He was?

Warmth filled her. Nobody had ever told her they were proud of her before. And to hear it coming from Jed meant a lot.

She yawned and his eyes grew even softer. Damn, she liked that. Also liked the way he called her babe. With a touch of affection in his voice. She didn't know what had happened between the other night and now. And she wasn't going to risk it by asking too many questions.

"You're tired." He reached for her coat, quickly undoing it and hanging it in the closet as though he'd done it a hundred times before.

"Are you hungry? You didn't eat any dinner." He glanced down at his watch. "After eleven now."

"He had to finish watching a game," she told him. "That's why we couldn't meet until later."

A disgusted look crossed his face. "Seriously? That guy was a dickhead. What kind of man puts his own desires before a woman?"

Most men, she figured. But she didn't say that either.

He took hold of her hand and led her into the kitchen. As though this wasn't her house and she didn't know where she was going. Maybe that should have annoyed her. But she kind of liked it. She liked the caring feeling to it. When he reached the small kitchen, he turned and picked her up, placing her on one of the kitchen stools.

"Right, babe. What do you feel like eating?"

Before she could stop him, he opened the fridge door.

Silence. Frown lines developed on his forehead, making him even more gorgeous if that was possible. Boy, her body couldn't handle it if he got too much sexier. She might just self-combust.

"I'm really not hungry," she told him. "Maybe I should just. . ."

She went to slide off her stool when he turned to scowl at her. "Sit right there."

Well, crap. He was using a new voice. An *I-mean-business* voice. She wasn't sure she liked it.

Don't kid yourself, you like it. You lap his dominant side up like a cat with a bowl of cream. With a big, fat smile on your face.

He walked over to the pantry, nearly pulled the doors off their hinges. She had to bite back a protest, figuring she shouldn't waste her breath. Her tummy tightened into a knot.

"Daisy," he spoke in a very low voice. Hmm, she didn't think that was a good sign. She looked over at the door, judging whether she could reach it before he caught her.

"Yes?" She shifted her gaze back to find him staring straight at her. She froze, caught. His eyes were a deep hazel-green normally, but right now she didn't even notice the color, she was intent on the emotion.

He did not look happy.

"Where is your food?"

"It's in there. And there's some in the fridge."

"There's milk in the fridge."

"There's also butter. And some bread in the freezer."

His eyebrows rose. "Bread in the freezer?"

She shrugged. "I'm one person. I can't eat a whole loaf before it gets all moldy so I keep it in the freezer."

He stalked back to the freezer. "That's all there is in here. And there is nothing in your pantry."

"There is too!" she replied hotly.

He turned the death-glare on her again. She swallowed heavily.

"You could have gotten a job for the Death Squadron," she muttered.

"What?"

She blushed. Whoops. She hadn't meant for him to hear that. She cleared her throat. "Nothing."

"Daisy, I don't like the word 'nothing'."

"Well, that seems a bit word-ist."

"What?"

"What did the word 'nothing' ever do to you?" *Okay, stop now, Daisy. This conversation is ridiculous.*

"When I ask a question, I want a proper answer, not an evasive one."

Shit. Yeah, she loved that dominant voice.

She cleared her throat. "I was just commenting that you could get a job with the Death Squadron because your glare is like a laser beam incinerating everything in its path, that's all. . .and now I feel like the biggest dork ever."

"You're not a dork." His eyes had grown tender as he stared at her. His face filled with warmth.

Wow. Just wow.

Now she was completely falling under his spell. Because while she liked his dominant side, she totally loved it when he went all tender and sweet. She closed her eyes for a moment against old memories that threatened to rush her. Of him leaning over her as she lay on a blanket, staring up at the blue sky, his eyes filled with love and affection. Him promising to be there for her always. Holding her as she cried when he told her he had to leave.

"Baby. Hey, you all right? What's wrong?"

He grasped hold of her shoulders, turning her and she opened her eyes to look up at him. *Baby*. That was even better than babe.

"The other night you looked at me like you didn't even know

me, like I was nothing. . .it hurt so bad. And now you're looking at me like you used to and I don't know what to do with that!"

"Oh, baby. It's been a rough few days for you, hasn't it?" He drew her against his chest and she cuddled in, letting the scent of him wrap around her, soothe her even as her insides danced in excitement.

"You really forgive me without even knowing everything?"

He was silent for a moment. "I don't like what you did. Still don't. But yeah, I can put it behind me."

Was putting it behind him the same as forgiving her? She wasn't sure. While part of her wanted to tell him the truth of what happened ten years ago, she figured all that would do is hurt him. And she'd hurt him enough.

"These past few nights, all I could think of was you. The memory of your eyes, filled with hurt because of me. The scent of you, the idea of how it would feel to have your legs around my hips while I took you deep. These thoughts kept me up at night. Then when I got home to hear you'd done something damn stupid like go on a date with some stranger." He blew out a breath. "It cemented what I already had playing on my mind. That I needed to see you. That I needed to feel those legs wrapped around me, have your scent filling my lungs."

"You want me."

"I want you."

Was it just about sex? She didn't know how she felt about that. On the one hand, she wanted to take it and run with it. She'd take whatever she could get. . .but she wanted it all.

Don't ask. Don't ruin this. Because you want him too. It's always been him for you.

"Can feel you've gone all tense. What is it, babe?" His hand was at her ass, squeezing and damn, that felt nice.

"Is. . .is it just about sex?"

She felt him stiffen. Shit. She shouldn't have asked. "Sorry, I shouldn't have—"

"It could never be about sex with you Daisy-girl."

That had been his nickname for her years ago and tears entered her eyes at the sound of it.

"Oh. Good." She leaned her forehead against his chest. Dork.

"Yeah. Good." He sounded amused. Then he wrapped his hand in her hair and pulled her head back. He kissed her. And Jesus, it was nothing like she'd experienced before. Her body melted into his, her lips parting for his tongue.

He wasn't making promises or declarations of love. She wasn't expecting that. They were both different people now who had to get to know each other. But he was here and he wasn't staring at her like she was nothing to him. So, she wanted to give him what he needed.

Although she wasn't ready for sex. Not yet. There were still things to tell him about her. Things he needed to know before that. And then there were the bruises on her thigh. She needed to get rid of those first.

She leaned back, stepping away. "Um, Jed, I . . ."

"Relax, Daisy. Nothing's happening tonight. We get to know each other a bit first, yeah?"

She relaxed. "Yeah."

Not that she'd ever let him know everything. No way did a man want a woman who slept with a snuggly, sucked her thumb and enjoyed playing with building blocks. There was no way he or any man would feel comfortable with that part of her.

But she'd lock that down tight. She knew she had to.

"Do you still want to get to know me? After I was a jerk?"

She'd take him any way she could. It was then that she realized she'd never gotten over Jed Carson. There was some reason she'd never dated, and part of that had been her life. Most of it had been because of this man.

"Of course, I do." She nodded so hard that her neck started to hurt.

"Easy, baby." He slid his hand around to the back of her neck. "I'm glad you still want that. But I feel I should warn you, I'm a very dominant guy. I like to make the rules. I don't want to sound like a jerk, I'm not going to tell you what to wear or that you can't talk or go out with your friends. But if you want to go out, I want to know where you're going and when you'll be back. Who you'll be with. Just so I can know you're good."

"Well, I don't have any friends here anyway." Or anywhere. But she didn't want to admit that and sound like a complete loser.

His eyes narrowed. "You have Ellie."

She nibbled her lip. "She's nice to me because I'm renting her house but. . ."

"Ellie likes you. She's your friend. She wouldn't be this friendly just because you're her tenant."

"Oh."

"And I have no doubt you'll make other friends."

She wasn't so sure. You actually had to leave the house in order to make friends. That's what she'd been trying to do tonight and look what had happened.

Disaster.

But she didn't need to tell Jed any of that. So, she nodded.

"If you have any trouble, I want to be the first person you call. I know there will be times when I won't be around because of work." He frowned slightly. "I'll figure something else out then."

"I wouldn't worry, I never get in trouble."

He raised his eyebrows. "You were in trouble tonight."

She frowned. "The only trouble I was in was being bored to tears by Moany Mike."

"You didn't notice the stares you were getting, did you?"

Stares? She looked at him questioningly. What was he talking about? He shook his head and tucked her hair behind her ears.

"My little innocent. Baby girl, there were at least half a dozen men watching you in that bar, and believe me, their hunger had nothing to do with that gristly piece of steak on your plate."

What? Was he serious? She shook her head. "I'm sure that's not true."

His face turned dark. Cold. "Believe me, they were."

Yikes. Okay, she wanted the sweet, soft look back. Because frankly, this hard Jed kind of scared her. Not that she was worried he would hurt her, but he looked like he wanted to go back to that bar and go all gonzo on those guys who were looking at her.

Not that she believed they were actually checking her out. Maybe they were staring at Mike. Watching him eat was pretty gross, though, she couldn't imagine anyone wanting to look at him while he did that. Ick.

"You think you can deal with the rules I gotta give you so I can sleep easy at night?"

Well, when he put it like that. . .she nodded. "Yes."

"Good girl." There was that warm look again. Jesus, she'd agree to just about anything to put that look on his face. He ran a thumb over her cheek. "I'm probably gonna lean towards being overly protective of you."

He had to stop saying things like that. She was about to burst into tears.

"Is this really happening?" she whispered.

"It is." His thumb rubbed under her eye. "You're tired, aren't you? You not been sleeping?"

She shook her head.

"What's your bedtime?"

Bedtime?

"Um, I usually just go to bed when I get tired."

"Hmm, way I remember it, you were a night owl. That still the case?"

She shrugged. "Guess so. I keep my own hours for my job so I can work when I like. I don't have to be up early."

"What do you do?"

"I'm an editor. Authors send me their books to edit."

"That's awesome. English was always your favorite subject."

"Yeah." She smiled at him shyly. "So as long as I have my laptop and internet, I'm set."

"Staying up all night might have suited you in the past, but you got to get more sleep, baby. I have to work tomorrow, but I'll bring over some food and cook us some dinner." He sighed and looked back at her kitchen with a shake of his head. "There's nothing in your cupboards but sweets and chocolate."

"And bread and butter and milk," she protested.

He just gave her a look. "You think that covers the food groups?" He strode to the pantry and pulled out a bag of gummy bears. "This is not real food."

"Hey, there's real fruit juice in those gummies. Says it on the packet."

"This is not the same as eating fruit," he growled at her.

"Well, maybe I'm just stocking up for Halloween."

He eyed the candy in the pantry. "You expecting the entire state of Montana to come knocking on your door?"

"There's not that much in there."

He grunted. "We need to have a chat about proper nutrition."

Yay. She couldn't wait. That sounded like so much fun.

"Don't pout, baby. It can't be good to live on sugar alone. Hate to think what you're doing to your teeth."

So did she. Which is why she tried not to think about it. It was also why she avoided going to the dentist. Ever. That and she was scared. Totally chicken shit scared.

"Do you want some toast before you go to bed?" he asked.

"No, I'm not really hungry."

"All right then. Let's get you into bed. I've got to get home and sleep too."

"You could stay here," she said shyly. Then she realized how that might have sounded. "The spare bedroom is all made up, I mean. So, you don't have to drive back so late."

"Thanks, but I start work early and I don't want to wake you up. Come on." He held out his hand to her and they made their way up the stairs. She thought it a bit odd that he wanted to come up with her. Nerves started dancing in her stomach. He wasn't coming into her bedroom, was he?

"Um, don't you need to get going?"

"Yep. Soon. This your bedroom?" He unerringly moved to her bedroom door. She nodded, not really thinking and was shocked as he walked inside. Okay, then. Jed Carson was in her bedroom.

Holy shit. He was in her bedroom!

She darted inside to find him standing by the bed, looking around at the mess. He glanced over at her. Most of her wardrobe was strewn around the room.

"Umm, sorry, I couldn't decide what to wear." She started picking up pants and tops and shoving them back in the wardrobe.

"Looks like a hurricane erupted in here," he said in amazement.

Why hadn't she cleaned up before she'd left? Oh yeah, because she'd been running late. But she could at least have made up the bed this morning.

He shook his head, luckily looking more amused than horrified. "Go get into your pjs and get ready for bed. I'll tidy this up."

Feeling mortified, she snatched up her pajamas off the floor where she'd chucked them this morning and high-tailed it into the bathroom. It didn't feel right leaving Jed in her bedroom. By himself. With her mess. But she also needed a few minutes to get her head on straight.

Jed was in her house.

He was in her bedroom.

He wanted to get to know her better.

He'd kissed her.

It had been spectacular. So much better than she'd remembered. She grinned into the mirror.

He had rules. Her face grew serious.

He really didn't like her eating habits. She frowned.

Hmm. There was one thing she knew about the new Jed. He was a force to be reckoned with. She had no doubts he was used to getting his own way. And she wondered exactly what that meant for her. She got changed then brushed her teeth. All she could do was see where this went.

She'd just have to do her best not to fuck it up.

JED TIDIED up the bedroom with some amusement and a little bit of horror. For someone who hated his cutlery being out of place, this could be an adjustment. Obviously, Daisy wasn't terribly concerned about putting things away. Although everything was clean, just in a bit of a mess.

He got her clothes quickly hung up in the wardrobe and into drawers then turned his attention to the bed. He wondered if he should check on her. She was taking a while in the bathroom. But then, women did, didn't they?

He studied her bed. It was large with a wrought-iron headboard which she'd twisted more fairy lights through.

He pulled back the covers and something flew off, landing on the floor near his feet. He frowned as he stared down at the piece of worn cloth. He picked it up. Faded and soft, it looked like a rag. But why would a rag be in her bed? He drew it to his nose. It smelled like her. Something stirred his memory. An image. Didn't she have an old blanket like this as a child? Was this what was left? That was sweet.

He wondered if she slept with it? For comfort?

He stared over at the door musingly, thinking about the abundance of candy in the kitchen. Didn't mean she was a Little.

What if she was? Well, that changed things. His plan had been to get her more comfortable with him. Get her into bed. Get her out of his head. How was he going to approach this, though? If she was, then she might not know it. Or not want him to know since she had no idea of what he was. Should he bring it up with her? Or test her?

She was so jumpy and unsure. And he didn't blame her after the way he'd acted. He didn't feel like the straight-forward approach was quite right. At least not yet.

So, he tucked the piece of blanket under the pillow and quickly made the bed as he heard her open the bathroom door.

"Oh." She paused as she entered the bedroom. "You really didn't have to tidy up."

He shrugged. He kind of did. That mess. . .well, it would have driven him nuts to leave it.

"And you made the bed." Her eyes widened and he saw her looking frantically around. Probably for the bit of blanket. Which was more of an indication that it was something special to her. Something she didn't want him knowing about.

"Come on," he said gently, watching her closely. "Let's get you all tucked in."

Before he'd seen that piece of blanket, he'd intended to just kiss her and leave before she climbed into bed. Not now. He held up the blankets. Waited for her to protest. She looked from him to the bed.

"In you get," he ordered, deliberately using his Dom voice.

She didn't even hesitate. She climbed in. Let him tuck the blankets around her.

All right. This didn't mean anything. She was probably in a bit of shock. And she might be submissive without being a Little.

He sat next to her, staring down at her. She gaped up at him with wide eyes. He reached up and fingered the fairy lights twisted through the rungs of the headboard. "You always loved fairy lights."

She relaxed slightly. "I know. They're so pretty. And there's something about them that's comforting. Whenever I look at them, I feel happy."

He wondered if she'd kept the lights, he'd given her so many years ago. Of course not. No doubt they'd died a long time ago.

He stared down at her. "Want a bedtime story?"

Her expressive eyes went even wider. She shook her head.

"Probably just as well," he muttered. "Not sure I know any."

"You don't?" Suddenly she grinned. "Maybe I should tell you one about the princess and the dragon."

"Oh yeah? Dragon, huh? I suppose he turns into a handsome prince with a kiss or after finding love or something like that."

"Oh no, this dragon is always a dragon. Breathing fire and stomping around bad-temperedly."

"That so?" He narrowed his gaze at her in mock-warning, loving the way her eyes danced with amusement. Even if it was at his expense.

He could take it. Especially if it put that carefree look on her face. When he'd known her, her life had been hard. He wondered how life had been since? What she'd been doing? Why she left him?

"Jed? You okay?"

He forced himself to smile down into her worried look. "Of course. So, is he a handsome dragon?"

"Oh yes, very handsome. But very grumpy. And bossy."

"Sometimes a dragon has to be bossy in order to keep his princess safe and happy."

She sighed, but a smile danced at the corner of her lips. "Yeah, dragons are good protectors." She turned to her side and yawned. "That's why I've always liked them."

He ran his fingers through her hair, massaging her scalp gently as he reached over and turned off the lamp. This left only the fairy lights she had strung along her headboard glowing.

He guessed she didn't like the pitch-black.

Lots of people don't. Doesn't mean anything.

No, but things were adding up.

A small snore escaped and he had to grin. His baby was tired. He leaned in and brushed his lips across her forehead. He liked that she felt comfortable enough to fall asleep with him here. It worried him that she might be too trusting, she didn't know him anymore.

He sat and just watched her sleep. She let out a low murmur, her forehead crinkling. He knew he should leave. He had to get up early. He needed to get some rest himself. But it was hard to tear himself away from the gorgeous image she made. Making a sudden decision, he reached under the pillow next to her and grabbed out her blankie, tucking it in next to her hand. He froze as she moved, hoping he hadn't woken her.

But she simply grabbed the piece of blanket and tucked it in under her nose, rubbing it back and forth in a gesture that made the hard wall around his heart melt slightly. He had to harden it back up.

Her thumb slipped into her mouth and his heart nearly stopped. All right then. Suddenly, he realized exactly what he was doing. She wasn't going to be happy if she woke and found him watching her like this.

He slowly stood and leaning down, lightly pressed his lips to her forehead. "Sleep well, baby girl. Daddy will be back tomorrow."

Calling himself Daddy felt right. More right than he should let it be until he knew for sure that was what she wanted.

6

S he was a mess.

She'd been a bundle of nerves all day. She hadn't been able to sit still. So instead of getting any work done, she'd spent the day cleaning and tidying.

She didn't want him to think she was a pig after seeing her bedroom last night.

But he'd have to actually turn up for him to see how tidy the house is.

She stared at the clock. It was after six. He wasn't coming. Something had turned him off. Maybe it was falling asleep while he was still in her bedroom. Crap. Had she done something while she was sleeping? What if she'd snored? Talked in her sleep? Sucked her thumb?

She froze at that thought. Shit. Why hadn't she thought of that until now? She paced up and down the living room, her hand on her rolling tummy. When she'd woken up this morning, she'd been holding her blankie, her thumb in her mouth as usual. What if he'd found her blankie? Seen her acting like a child?

No man wanted that.

Yep, she'd totally fucked this all up. She was such a dork. An idiot.

She sunk down onto the sofa feeling completely dejected when the doorbell rang.

Maybe it was the sexy bras and panties she'd ordered. She'd never owned anything sexy in her life, but if she was going to start dating, she couldn't exactly wear her princess panties and white cotton bras.

She opened the door without looking, expecting the delivery man to be on the other side.

But there stood Jed. Two bags of groceries in his arms and a scowl on his face.

"What are you doing here?" she asked breathlessly.

His eyebrows rose. "Did you forget that I was coming over tonight?"

"Uh, no, I just, I thought that maybe you weren't. . .it's after six."

He nodded. She noticed then that behind the scowl he was wearing that he looked tired. "Sorry. I should have called. I worked later than I thought I would. Have you eaten?"

"What? No, I haven't. Oh, come in."

Daisy, get yourself together.

He stepped forward, but he stopped when he was standing right in front of her. He looked from the door to her. Umm, what did he want?

"I'll lock the door," she said suddenly, remembering his words from last night.

"You look to see who it was before you opened the door?"

Her breath caught in her throat. Um. Uh-oh. By the very serious look on his face as he asked that she got the feeling he was not going to like hearing her answer.

"Because there's no peephole. Which means you need to look

through the side window. I didn't see you looking through the side window."

And of course, he would notice. The damn man saw everything.

"I knew you were coming," she said hastily. Whew. Good excuse.

But the look on his face said he wasn't buying that one. "Seems to me you thought I wasn't turning up. Also seems to me that you should be checking anyway, even if you do think it's me, that doesn't mean it is. That's another rule."

She was going to need to get these written down. Before she could question him, though, he'd taken off down the hall towards the kitchen.

Okay, then. She hastily shut and locked the door. When she reached the kitchen, he was already unpacking bags.

Her eyes widened as she took in all the food. "How many people you cooking for?"

He snorted. "This ain't all for tonight. This is for you to eat over the next week."

"Week? This is enough to last me a month."

He shot her a look. "Well, since you won't be filling up on sweets and chocolate, I expect you'll be able to eat most of this."

Umm, say what now?

She frowned over at him. "If I need groceries, I can just order them online." That sounded a bit bitchy and ungrateful. But he didn't get mad. He just continued to unpack. She sighed.

"You don't like going to the grocery store yourself?" he asked.

She didn't really like going anywhere. She knew she should make more of an effort to get out. But the trip to Sanctuary Ranch and last night's disastrous date had shown her that getting out and about was overrated.

"Not particularly," she told him. "You really shouldn't have bought all this."

"I like to eat."

"I can see that." She looked him over. You didn't get muscles like that from living on air.

"You like what you see?" he asked.

Her eyes widened. "Nope."

He froze.

"I really, really like what I see." Then she blushed. She sounded like a complete dork. Jesus, she wished she knew how to talk to men. She'd never had a problem talking to Jed back when they were teenagers. But she was hugely out of practice. "You know, you're okay."

He grinned. "Okay, huh? I can see I might have to add some time to my work out."

"You really don't," she said hastily. "Really. You're perfect."

"Nobody is perfect."

She wasn't so sure about that. Because when she looked at him, she didn't see a single flaw. The man was ripped. Sexy. Strong. While not classically handsome, he had the sort of face that caught your attention and held it. That was if you could get your eyes off the rest of his body.

"Hope you're hungry. We're having steak, mashed potatoes and spinach for dinner."

Spinach. Ick.

"I take it from that look that there's something you don't like in that list."

"Spinach is gross."

"You'll try it."

She shook her head. "Nope. I've tried it before. Yuck."

He just gave her a look. "How long since you've had it?"

"Umm." Truth or lie? Maybe something in between. "Can't remember, but I remember it was like eating slime."

He rolled his eyes. "I promise it won't taste like slime."

She felt her lower lip drop out.

"And no pouting or you don't get any ice cream afterwards."

Hey! That wasn't cool. But she quickly stopped her pout. Then she thought about what just happened.

"I'm an adult," she pointed out.

He ran his gaze over her, leaving a wave of heat in his wake. "Yep. You sure are."

"So, you can't take away my dessert."

"I'm cooking so it's my rules."

Well, that sucked meatballs. Hmm, meatballs sounded quite good. Maybe she could convince him to make meatballs and spaghetti. No disgusting vegetables in sight.

"Maybe we should have meatballs," she suggested. "I could go get some ground beef." What was she doing? Did she really want to go to the grocery store right now? With Jed here, in her house?

That was a big fat nope.

Jed turned and looked at her. "You like meatballs?"

"Sure," she said happily.

"All right, I'll cook them another night. Tonight, we're having steak, spinach and mashed potatoes."

She sighed. Long and loud. She saw his mouth twitch, but his gaze remained stern.

"So, when I cook it's my rules?"

"Nope," he replied as he peeled potatoes.

"That's not fair."

His eyes crinkled, but he didn't crack a smile. She might just make it her mission in life to make him smile.

He reached over and tapped her nose with his finger. "I let you cook; we'll probably be eating fish sticks with a side of gummy worms."

He wasn't wrong.

"I can cook," she told him. She'd had to learn how. She didn't much like it, though. And now that she no longer had younger siblings to take care of, she had figured she didn't much have to worry about creating balanced meals.

"Babe, can tell from your voice you don't much like cooking, am I right?"

"I pretty much detest it," she replied. "I cooked dinner every night for years, with vegetables. Then once Brad and Sylvie left me, I figured I didn't have to bother anymore. So, I don't."

"Left you?" he asked quietly.

Danger. Danger. Back away from that one.

"I mean when they moved out."

"What about your mom? Where was she?" he asked.

"She bailed on us soon after we left."

"How come you guys didn't get taken into foster care after she bailed?" He didn't look at her. If he did, he probably would have noticed the way she'd frozen. She thought he didn't want to talk about the past. Nerves fluttered in her stomach making her feel ill.

"I told everyone I was twenty," she told him. "I got a fake ID and we made sure we stayed out of trouble so no one paid much attention."

He nodded and changed the subject. "You don't like cooking, luckily I do. Don't always get the chance and I won't always be here to do it. But I got you some frozen meals. When I have more time, I'll cook some meals to go in the freezer."

"You don't have to do that," she whispered.

"Babe, you're living on sugar and caffeine, if I don't do something, you're going to get sick. It's a wonder you have any immune system left."

"I don't really go anywhere to get sick," she protested.

Crap. When was she going to learn to guard what she said?

"You were out last night, weren't you?"

Took every ounce of courage she had to do that and then she'd nearly chickened out several times.

"Why don't you like going out?" he asked in a soft voice. "Daisy? Look at me, please."

It was the 'please' that did it. Then when she glanced up and saw the soft look on his face, she kind of melted. Total and utter goo.

"Yes?"

"Why don't you like going out? You got a phobia about leaving the house?"

"Not that." She sighed. "It's just a bit scary, I guess." She glanced down at her finger as she drew a pattern on the kitchen counter.

"Scary?" he prompted.

She shrugged, wishing she hadn't admitted that. She was such a wimp.

Little whore. You'll never amount to anything.

Crap. Crap.

"Daisy. Daisy," he said more sharply. She looked up into his hazel eyes which were filled with concern. "That's better. Where did you just go?"

"Nowhere."

"All right. We need to get a few things straight. Thought I made things clear last night, seems I didn't." He was putting food on both plates and her stomach actually growled. It looked pretty good. Except for the spinach. Gross.

"Come on, grab some cutlery and let's eat at the dining table and we can chat."

"Do we have to chat?"

Jed snorted as they both took a seat. "Think I've spoken more to you tonight than I have to anyone else in the past week."

That didn't surprise her. He didn't strike her as the verbose type. But he had no problem talking to her.

She picked up her fork and dug into the mashed potatoes. Damn, they were cooked perfect. Light, fluffy and buttery.

"Want me to cut up your steak for you?" he asked suddenly.

She froze. Stared at him with another forkful of mashed potatoes halfway to her mouth. Her mouth was open. She slammed it shut. *That probably looked real attractive, Daisy.* The potatoes slid off the fork and landed on her lap. Shit.

She sighed. "Crap."

But instead of looking disgusted by her or making a smart-assed comment, Jed just stood.

"Don't swear," he scolded mildly. "Wait there, I'll get a cloth."

He returned quickly with a cloth, but when she reached for it, he pulled it back. She looked up at him with hurt. Was he playing some kind of game?

"Hey," he said gently, reaching out to take hold of her chin. "I'll clean you up, all right?"

"Why?" she asked.

"Because I want to take care of you." He used the cloth to tidy her up. "I enjoy it."

Her heart raced. "You used to take care of me."

He sat with a nod, putting the cloth down on the table. "I did."

"Not like that."

"Not sure we ever ate mashed potatoes together."

"You know what I mean."

He stared at her straight on. "I do know what you mean. Back then we were kids, but I always knew I wanted to look after you. Nobody else ever did."

She flinched at that, even though it was nothing less than the truth. He reached out again and gently raised her chin so she had to look at him. "Didn't say that to hurt you, sugar."

"I know." She tried to smile, but failed miserably. "It's just the truth. My mom never even noticed I existed and I spent most of my time looking after Brad and Sylvie. You were the only person who ever watched out for me."

And then she left him. And nothing had been the same since.

She saw something flash through his eyes and his hand dropped. Her heart raced with fear. Was he remembering too? Remembering the promises they'd made to each other? Promises she'd broken.

"Jed—"

"Eat your dinner," he said abruptly.

"Jed—"

"Daisy, eat."

A lump developed in her throat. Suddenly, her appetite was gone.

"Eat your dinner, Daisy."

"I can't. I don't feel so great."

He stared at her for a moment, she expected him to scold her or maybe get a bit impatient. Instead, he surprised her by reaching over and pulling her into his lap. She froze. She'd been in his lap before, as a teenager. But this Jed was a whole different experience. He was firm, large, and hard. She wiggled around.

He gave her a light slap on the side of her thigh that had her stilling. "Sit still."

"I'm on your lap."

"So you are," he said in a lighter voice.

"Why?"

"I wanted you close." He reached over and pulled her plate towards him. He'd eaten everything on his plate. He started cutting up her steak.

"I can do that," she said quickly, reaching for the knife and fork. He gave her hand a light slap.

"Put your hands down."

"But—"

"I caused you to get upset so you lost your appetite, now it's my job to settle you down so you can eat."

She wasn't sure how she felt about that statement. Except, if he thought holding her on his lap would settle her down, he was delusional.

"I can sit in my own chair," she said a little desperately.

"Nope, you can sit right here."

Her temper stirred. "Anybody ever tell you that you're far too bossy?"

"Yep," he said with a grin. "Now, open up." He held up a fork with a small piece of steak and some potatoes on it to her mouth. Now this was going too far. She reached for the fork and he drew it back with a sigh.

Then he stood and set her down on her seat. "Okay, this is the way it's going to go. You're going to keep your hands palm up on your thighs while I feed you dinner. Each time you move your hands, it's two spanks."

Umm, what? Seriously?

"You're joking."

"I'm not. You up for it?"

She just stared at him. He didn't smile or wink like it was a joke and she remembered what he'd said last night. "Do you like doing that, spanking women?"

"Sometimes, I do."

"And you think I need that? To be. . .spanked."

"I think for too long you've been the one in charge. Doing everything. Making the decisions. For right or wrong. And now you're on your own. And you need watching over so you don't eat yourself into a sugar coma or go out with complete strangers to dangerous bars. Remember how I said there was gonna be rules? Well, with rules there are always consequences for breaking them, otherwise what's to hold you to them, right? And the consequences have to be such that it will make you think twice before breaking those rules."

"And the consequence is a spanking?"

"You ever been spanked?"

"No. Never." Her mother would have had to notice her to do that. "I don't think there were ever any rules, other than don't interrupt her while she was working." She made a face.

"There were rules for your siblings, though, right? That you made."

"Yeah."

"And you enforced those rules."

She wrinkled her nose as she thought back. "Not very well."

"I can see how that would be hard for you." He studied her. "Taking a disciplinarian role wouldn't come naturally to you. Being in charge is what I need. While we're together, keeping you safe and healthy is my job. I take that very seriously."

While they were together?

She felt ill at the thought that he didn't think this would last.

How would she ever lose him again? She was already falling fast and hard. Hell, she'd never really fallen out of love with him. Sylvie thought she was crazy. That her feelings for him couldn't be real. That she'd made him into something in her head that wasn't real. In part, she was right. In her head, he'd been someone else. But he was also so much more than she'd imagined.

There were no promises. All she could do was hope. Hope that he might find that love for her that he'd once had. Although part of her worried he never would. Not when he didn't know everything.

But maybe he was right and it was for the best the past stayed there.

He ran his thumb along her lower lip. "Hey, look at me. If you can't do this, we can think of other consequences. It's important that you don't fear me. I would never do anything to hurt you or scare you, you believe that right?"

"I know you wouldn't." If anything, he was too protective, her dragon.

"You followed my lead in the past. Maybe not to this extent and

I know we're both different. I'm more dominant, more take-charge." He tilted his head, studying her. "And I almost think you're more in need of guidance than you were before."

He wasn't wrong. She felt lost. Adrift. She had since Sylvie and Brad left.

"Yeah, that's what I thought." He glanced down at her plate. "While I feed you this, you think about whether or not you want to accept my consequences."

Wow. Generous of him to give her a minute or two to think. But was there much to think about? He was the only person she'd ever truly trusted, but she'd been taught over and over that people were assholes.

Not Jed.

Still, she wasn't sure about all this. She didn't know this Jed well.

"Baby, in order to eat you need to open your mouth."

She opened her mouth slowly and he slipped the piece inside.

"And now you chew."

She chewed obediently.

"It was too soon, wasn't it?" he asked.

"Yeah," she breathed out, glad he understood.

The skin around his eyes crinkled and she felt the tension in her drain away. "Yeah. I get that. You don't know me well and I'm comin' on strong."

That was it exactly.

She nodded her head.

"So, we'll defer punishment."

What did that mean? As she opened her mouth to ask, he fed her another forkful of steak.

"You misbehave, earn yourself punishment, then I'll keep a tally. When you're ready to submit to my discipline then we'll deal with it. Might be one hell of a spanking, though. Unless you got a real problem with being spanked."

She thought that over for a moment. Her over his lap, her butt bare, feeling his hand crack down on the bare skin. She'd edited a few books with spanking scenes and they never failed to turn her on. Her heart raced with nerves and excitement and shockingly she felt her clit throb. She pressed her thighs together. That just made it ache even more.

He grinned. "You ain't got a problem with being spanked."

"I didn't say that."

"Part of my job is being observant." He tapped her nose. "You might want to remember that next time you try to lie to me."

"I don't lie," she muttered.

He stiffened for a moment then the tension eased out of him. "Evasive answers are something I consider a lie. When I ask a question, I like an answer in return. Or if you can't answer for some reason, I want you to tell me that. I probably won't like that, but it's better than saying nothing is wrong when something is. All right?"

"All right." She guessed she could deal with that. The rest of it. . .shit, he'd given her a lot to think over.

He fed her a forkful of potatoes. Some of them smeared on her lip and she reached over to grab the cloth.

"Uh-uh, where is your hand meant to be," he chided.

Her hand slammed down to her thigh. Shoot. She glanced up at him, but instead of looking annoyed, his eyes were dancing.

"Relax, baby. This isn't serious. It's a game. When it's serious, you'll know."

A game?

"So, you're not really going to spank me?"

"Oh no, you just earned yourself two. But whatever the tally reaches by the end of the meal, it won't be a hard spanking. Course, break my other rules and that's a different story."

He wiped her mouth himself. Jeez, when was the last time someone had done that?

She took another bite. She was starting to get full and she wasn't even a fourth of the way through the plate of food.

This time he held up a forkful of spinach. He looked from the fork he held to her and she swore this devilish look crossed his face. "Want me to do the choo-choo train?"

Her eyes widened. "You wouldn't."

Oh, she should have known better than to say that.

He pulled his hand back. "Here comes the choo-choo train. Choo! Choo!"

She tried to frown at him, she really did. But it was so ridiculous. This big, serious man who probably knew thirty ways to kill a person and get away with it, was doing the choo-choo train. She found herself bursting into laughter.

And she finally got that smile she'd been waiting for. It was fleeting. There one second, gone the next. But it had been there, and her heart grew lighter. She even ate a mouthful of the damn spinach. Then wished she could spit them out. With a grimace, she swallowed them down then jumped up and raced into the kitchen to grab a can of pop from the fridge to wash down the slimy taste.

"Getting out of your seat is ten," he called out.

Damn it.

7

If anyone had told him a week ago that he'd be sitting on a couch with Daisy tucked up against him, watching some reality TV cooking show, he'd have thought them delusional. But he was here. With her.

His girl.

After she'd jumped up to grab some pop to wash down the spinach, he hadn't made her eat anymore. He had insisted on a few more mouthfuls of steak and potatoes, though. He'd even let her have some ice cream. He'd have to watch or she'd have him wrapped around her little finger if he wasn't careful.

Although, she'd moaned so much about the small amount he'd given her, that he'd ended up tacking on ten more to her tally. Hmm, seemed his girl wouldn't sit well for a while come reckoning day if she kept this up.

He ran his hand up and down her arm. He didn't want to push her too hard too fast, last thing he wanted was for her to run. His body tightened at the thought. She'd done it before. Could do it again.

But he wasn't the boy he once was. He was going into this with his eyes wide open. This was about working her out of his system. And he also knew how to track things down. There was nowhere she could hide that he wouldn't find her. *If* he wanted to chase her.

"Jed? You all right?"

He stared down into those deep, gray eyes. His body stirred. The thought of lying down and pulling her over him, of getting those tight jeans off her, of stripping her naked and having her ride him or sit on his face so he could eat her out. . .fuck, he needed to stop. It was too soon.

"Need a bit of your sugar."

Her eyes widened.

"Right here." He pointed to his lips.

She licked her own lips. Looked hesitant. More hesitant than he would have thought. He narrowed his gaze. "You scared of kissing me?"

"I'm just not used to. . ." she trailed off, looking away.

Used to what? Surely Bobby had kissed her. He tensed, pushing that thought away. He was starting to have his doubts about how long Bobby had stuck around.

"I'm sorry I'm not very good at this. I'll try harder," she said in a rush, staring at him worriedly. He realized he was scowling and no doubt scaring her half to death.

"Sh, I'm not mad at you. I was thinking of something else. Come here." He tapped his lap then helped her climb over so she was facing him, her thighs straddling his. He ran his thumbs up her inner thighs, felt her shiver. Reaching up, he wrapped his hand around the back of her head and pulled her in for a light, gentle kiss.

Sugar and strawberries.

He moved his hands down her back, digging into tight spots he found.

"Jesus, you're wound up tight. When was the last time you had a massage?"

"Uh, I've never had one."

That bastard never gave her a massage?

"You must get sore working on a computer for long hours." He dug his fingers into her neck.

She groaned, her eyes fluttering shut. "I do."

"Poor baby, if I had more time, I'd give you a proper rub down."

Her eyes opened. "You have to leave now?" She sounded so disappointed that it made his insides melt.

"Soon," he told her, even though he should have left an hour ago. "I have to go out of town tomorrow. If I make it back, it will be late so I won't be able to come for dinner. But I expect you to eat one of those frozen meals, understand? I want you to send me a photo of you eating real food."

"I don't have your number."

He nodded. "Yeah, forgot to give it to you last night. Go get me your phone and I'll put it in."

She climbed off his lap and he couldn't help but give her ass a slap. She turned back, looking startled, her hand against her butt. "Brute." There was a glint of amusement in her eyes. She skipped over and grabbed her cell. She seemed to get a burst of energy at night.

He took her phone, programming in his number. "You sleep well last night?" He kept his voice light. Still, he noticed her tense and send him a suspicious look but he wasn't going to mention anything about the worn piece of blanket he'd found in her bed. Or the number of cues he'd picked up on tonight. But it was too soon to bring it up. He'd already thrown enough stuff at her.

He handed her back her phone.

"I did," she said quietly. "Sorry I fell asleep so quickly. I didn't do anything embarrassing did I?"

"Like what?"

Her eyes bounced off his. "I don't know, snore or something? I thought maybe I had when you didn't call me today. I figured maybe you'd decided not to come tonight."

Oh, poor baby.

He reached for her, tumbled her back into his lap and took a deeper drink of her lips this time, playing with her, building their arousal higher and higher before he had to pull back. Her eyes were dazed as she stared up at him dreamily. Damn, she was satisfying.

"I'd have been here first thing this morning if I could have. Before I go it's best you know the other rules, yeah? So, you can make sure to behave yourself."

"Yes." She watched him warily now.

"First is honesty. No lies between us. That includes evasive answers."

She nodded.

"Second is no running away without telling me. Something goes wrong, upsets you then you talk to me. Understand?"

Her eyes went wide. "I'm not going anywhere."

"Good." Although he wasn't sure he quite believed that. Yet.

"I said this last night, I'll say it again because it bears repeating. You get in trouble, you call me. Straight away."

"Not the police?"

"Depending on the situation, police first then me a close second. Clear?"

"Yes."

"Four is about safety. You check the door to see who's there first before you open it. We've already talked about you going out and what I expect."

"Okay," she answered.

"Five is eating habits. I don't want you to get sick and you're going to if you keep eating the way you do. You can't live on sugar and caffeine. You eat three real meals a day, understand me? Even if I'm not here to make sure you do that."

She wrinkled her nose. "Yes, I got that."

"Last, I don't make it back tomorrow night, I want a text before you go to bed. I'll call if I can to say goodnight."

"All right."

"And Daisy, what we got here, it's exclusive, understand me? There is no one else. Understand?"

HURT STABBED AT HER. He really thought she would do that to him? That she would see someone else on the side?

Of course, he does, because he thinks you cheated on him once. He's never going to trust you without the truth.

"Hey, I didn't say that to cause you pain. We were kids back then. Holding onto anger and hurt doesn't help anyone."

Yeah, she knew that. Possibly more than anyone.

Get yourself together, Daisy. He's here with you now. So what if he thinks you were a cheating slut?

Ouch. Ouch.

"Hey. Look at me." He raised her face, undoubtedly seeing the misery in her eyes. Even if he was misreading the cause. He probably thought she felt remorse. Well, she did. But not for the reason he thought.

She was not a whore.

Did you really think that I'd allow my grandson to get mixed up with white trash little slut like you?

Ouch. Ouch. Ouch. She pressed her nails into her palms, waiting for the pain to chase away the words.

"Daisy? Baby? Fuck."

Suddenly, she found herself pressed against hard, warm male. And the voice disappeared. Like magic. Wow. Okay. Maybe there was another cure for getting rid of the bad words and thoughts. The memories.

Jed.

He rubbed his hand up and down her back. "Hey, I didn't mean to hurt you, I just wanted everything to be clear. Fuck. I'm sorry, baby."

She wrapped her arms around him, hugging him tight, hating that he sounded so upset. This was her dragon. He was usually encased in steel but the idea of hurting her got through that tough shield of his.

And that was sweet as hell.

"I'm sorry too," she told him, her voice filled with emotion. She knew he wouldn't fully understand what for but as soon as she said it some of that weight lifted from her chest. She felt his arms loosen and worried for a moment that he would push her away. But he pulled her tight.

"Damn, how did I ever think I'd get over you?" he asked

"Um, I'm not sure if I'm meant to apologize or not for that?" she asked.

"No apologies, so long as you never got over me as well."

"I didn't," she whispered. "Not in all those years, a day didn't ever go by where I didn't think of you. Wish I could talk to you."

"You could have, you'd just picked up a phone," he growled, a hint of annoyance in his voice.

"But I—"

Instead of letting her talk, he pressed his mouth against hers.

"Don't remember you ever being this sweet. But I like it. Like that it's all mine. Mine." He wrapped his hand around the nape of her neck. "All fucking mine."

His. She'd always been his. Even if he was an over-protective, bossy, blunt dragon.

"I really have to go," he muttered. "Don't want to."

She didn't want him to either.

"You got any questions for me?"

"Yeah, do I get to make rules for you?"

His lips twitched. "You gonna be able to enforce them?"

She blushed bright red. "I could figure out a way."

"Most of those rules apply to me as well. It's about respect, communication and honesty."

"What about contacting me if you're in trouble?"

"Baby, no offense, but I'm in trouble, you're the last person I call."

Hurt filled her and she fought it down.

"Daisy, listen to me. I didn't say that to hurt you or because I don't trust you. But any trouble I'm in is probably due to my job, which means it could be dangerous. I protect you; I don't pull you into danger. Okay?"

"Yeah, okay." She guessed she got it. But this felt kind of one-sided to her.

He lifted her off him then stood. "I got to go before I turn into a pumpkin."

She giggled. "It was the carriage that turned into a pumpkin not Prince Charming."

"Prince Charming, huh? Not sure I've ever been called that." He leaned in and kissed her gently. "Been called a lot worse. Charlie and Ellie call me Rambo."

She studied him and nodded. "I get it." He was way more Rambo than Prince Charming. For sure.

He rolled his eyes. "Lock the door behind me then get to bed, understand?"

She saluted him.

"Smart ass." He gave her ass a slap then slipped his hand into the back pocket of her jeans as she walked him out. She liked that. A lot. He pulled on his jacket and boots then opened the door and strode onto the porch, shutting it behind him.

"Night, sugar," he called out.

"Good night, pumpkin," she called back.

8

She studied the contents of her wardrobe scattered around the bedroom. Jed had called to tell her he was taking her out for dinner tonight and to be ready when he got there. She rolled her eyes at his no-nonsense tone. She glanced at the clock and saw she had thirty minutes before he arrived. Why hadn't she asked him where they were going?

What if it was somewhere fancy? What if she didn't know how to act? What if she made a complete idiot of herself and embarrassed him?

Realizing she was on the point of hyperventilating, she forced herself to sit and take deep breaths.

Think, Daisy. This is Jed. He's not into fancy.

Right.

If you needed to dress up, he would have told you.

Maybe.

He wouldn't let you make a dick of yourself.

Her breathing calmed. Nope, he wouldn't do that. They'd been seeing each other again for less than a week, but one thing she had learned was he liked to take care of her. He was also too bossy for her own good. She winced thinking of what her tally was up to. He was far too interested in what she ate and how much sleep she got. She hadn't realized that men cared about things like that when it came to their girl-friends.

You don't know that you're his girlfriend. You don't know what you are.

She chewed at her lip. This wasn't helping her get ready. Finally, she picked up a pair of comfortably faded jeans, some kick-ass deep green boots that went just above her ankle, a green top that had a wide neck and flowed around her body. She'd take a jacket for the cooler weather.

She dressed and dabbed on some make-up then brushed her hair until it sparkled. Her phone rang and she picked it up off the bed. Unknown number.

"Hello?"

Nothing.

"Hello?" she asked again, getting annoyed if this was some scammer trying to get money from her, they were gonna get an earful. "Hello, are you there?"

Still nothing.

"Jerk! Don't call back." She ended the call and glared at her phone. Then the doorbell went and she forgot all about the call.

She raced down the stairs, and remembered at the last moment to check out the side window. Definitely didn't need to add to the tally she'd already accumulated. There he stood, dressed in jeans, boots, dark blue shirt that was tucked in and a jacket.

Whew. She'd dressed right.

She opened the door with a smile.

"Hey there, baby." He looked her up and down and his eyes showed that he liked what he saw.

"Come in, or do we have to get going?" she asked.

"Need to get moving." But he stepped forward. "First, though, I need my kiss."

He was big on kissing. He always insisted on her kissing him when he first saw her and when he left. She guessed it wasn't such a big deal to give him what he wanted.

Like you don't love every second of it.

He pressed his hands into the back pockets of her jeans and squeezed her ass as he took her mouth with his. He pulled back to study her. "Now that's what I'm talking about. You're looking damn beautiful."

"Thanks," she said shyly. Just in case tonight was the night he took things further; she was wearing her sexy new bra and panties and she'd shaved her pussy. The bruising had pretty much faded from her thigh, at least to the point she could just tell him she'd knocked into something. That part had been hard, making sure she didn't pinch herself. But she'd done it. Because she knew that was one conversation she definitely wasn't ready to have.

He wiped his thumb under her lower lip. "Smudged your make-up."

"I don't care."

Crinkles appeared around his smiling eyes. She sighed dreamily.

Okay, Daisy. Get yourself together.

"Get your jacket, baby. It's cold out," he bossed. "You got another cardigan or sweater or something to go over that top?"

"You don't like this top?" she asked.

"I fucking love this top." He ran his finger over her bared shoulder. "But I don't want you getting cold."

"You can keep me warm," she surprised herself by saying.

"I can. Other people in the restaurant might not like when I pull you onto my lap to cuddle you, though."

She grinned. "Maybe not. I'll be all right, though. I'm warm enough."

He frowned slightly. "Go get another top."

She sighed. Made certain it was long and loud. "You are entirely too bossy." But she turned to climb the stairs, jumping with a yelp as he slammed his hand on her ass.

"Hey, what was that for?"

"That sigh. It was very bratty. Bratty behavior gets an immediate response."

"Still haven't made my mind up about that," she grumbled as she made her way upstairs.

"Yes, you have," he called back, sounding almost cheerful.

The ass.

But she couldn't deny the delicious thrill that ran through her and as soon as she was out of sight, she cupped her ass cheek. Wow.

SHE LOOKED DOWN at the menu. He'd brought her to a steakhouse. A nice one. Not some sleazy bar like Moany Mike, who it seemed hadn't got the memo that she wasn't interested in him. He'd tried to contact her twice through the dating app. She'd finally taken herself off the site, deleting her profile. She didn't need it anymore and she didn't want Jed finding out that he was still trying to contact her. Last thing she wanted was Mike turning up dead in a ditch and Jed to end up doing life behind bars. She was way too chicken-shit to visit a prison.

"What do you feel like eating, baby?" Jed asked her.

Hmm, that was a good question. "Lasagna sounds good."

"Hi, what can I get you?" the waitress asked cheerfully, her gaze studying Jed hungrily.

She guessed she couldn't blame the other woman. Jed was gorgeous.

"Hey, I'll have a steak, medium rare. No sauce. Baked potato with the works. She'll have the lasagna and we'll both have salad on the side. Thanks."

She gaped at him as the waitress collected their menus. "I can order for myself."

"Yep," he agreed amicably. "But we both know you wouldn't have bothered ordering any salad if you had."

"I didn't want salad," she said with a pout.

He reached over and tapped his finger against her lower lip. "What happens to girls who pout?"

She immediately pulled her lip back. "Sometimes I think you forget I'm an adult."

He stared at her, the look in his eyes pure heat. Her breath caught. "Believe me, I don't forget that. But you can be an adult and a Little too."

"What does that mean?"

"I'll explain it later. Here isn't really the place." He ran his hand up her thigh.

Her breath caught. "Jed!"

He leaned over and kissed her neck. He nuzzled at her ear. Oh hell, who knew that could send a direct zing straight to her clit? Their food arrived and she stared at the salad with disgust, digging into the lasagna immediately. By the time she was half-way through, she was full.

Jed cleared his throat as she pushed her plate away, rubbing at her tummy. "That was yummy."

"Hope you left some room for your salad," he told her.

He took a sip of water. She'd ordered a pop, ignoring his glower.

"Oh, I forgot about that." She picked up her fork and ran it through the leaves. Maybe if she did that enough it would look like she'd eaten something.

"Sure, you did." He leaned in, kissed her earlobe. "Eat ten mouthfuls like a good girl and I'll give you a reward."

"And if I don't?"

"Then I'll be adding another twenty to your tally."

"Twenty!" She gaped at him.

"Yep."

She figured lettuce wasn't that bad. Rabbits ate it. Rabbits were cute.

"Babe," he said with amusement. "It's salad, not a bowl full of worms."

"Eew." She wrinkled her nose. "Why'd you have to go say that, now I'm wondering if they washed the salad properly. What if there are slugs in there?"

"You're so damn cute. Eat the salad. There are no slugs. I promise. Here, I'll check it for you." He pulled the bowl of salad towards him and ran the fork around it, checking all the lettuce over. "Slug-free. Scout's honor."

"You weren't a scout."

"I was. Grandfather insisted. I lasted a week before they asked me very politely to leave."

She grinned and placed a small forkful of salad in her mouth. Yeah, okay, it didn't taste that bad. In fact, the dressing they had on it was quite nice.

But she wasn't going to tell him that.

9

She stared at those last few forkfuls of chocolate mousse cake with a groan. "I can't believe I'm going to say this, but I don't think I can fit any more in."

Jed, who hadn't eaten dessert and was sipping on a coffee, raised his eyebrows. "Am I gonna need to carry you out of here?"

"Will you be embarrassed if I undo the top button on my jeans," she half-joked.

"Baby, you could never embarrass me."

Wow. That was sweet. And totally not true.

"Give me a chance, I'm sure I could."

His gaze was serious. "No, baby. You couldn't."

"What if I tripped, bumped into the waiter and he spilled red wine all over that woman's white dress?" She nodded over at a table where a woman in a very tight white dress sat eating.

"I'd pick you up, make sure you were unharmed then offer to pay for her dry-cleaning."

"All right." She thought for a few seconds. "What if I was wearing a flowy skirt and a gust of wind pushed it up, showing my panties to everyone?"

"I'd hold your skirt down for you until we were out of the wind."

She tapped her chin. "What if I slipped while we were walking down a hill and bowled you over and we both tumbled down to the bottom?"

"Then after I made certain you were all right; I'd check your footwear since you seem to be tripping a lot."

She rolled her eyes.

He reached across and took hold of her hand in his. "Baby, I could never be embarrassed by anything you could do or say. Trust me."

I won't have the embarrassment of having you in our family.

She sucked in a breath.

"Daisy? What's going on?" he asked astutely.

She forced herself to smile. "Sorry. Just thinking about something someone said to me."

"What was it?"

"It's in the past. The future is what counts, right?"

She could see he was unhappy, but he couldn't argue that since it was his dictate.

"You ready to go home?" he asked instead.

She nodded and he signaled the waiter for the bill. She reached for her handbag and pulled out her wallet. A big hand reached out and wrapped around her wrist. "What do you think you're doing?"

"Getting some cash for dinner?"

He raised one eyebrow. "I invited you out."

"Um, yes."

"You think when I invite you to dinner that I expect you to pay?" he grumbled, sounding seriously unhappy.

"Well, I wasn't sure. . ."

"Now you know, I invite you out, you don't pay. Got it?"

"I've got it. So, does that mean if I invite you out, then I pay?"

That seemed pretty fair. She slid her wallet back into her handbag. She'd bring him back here soon, so things were even.

"No, it doesn't."

She frowned at him as he pulled out his credit card. The waiter rushed over with the check, stopping her from saying anything. Once he'd paid, Jed stood and pulled her chair out.

Then he slid his hand into the back pocket of her jeans as he guided her out to get their jackets. He held out hers for her, waiting for her to slide her arms in before turning her and doing it up. She sucked in a breath at the act.

He did it right up to the top then tapped her nose. "Can see there's a lot going on in that mind of yours, babe."

"It would be fairer if you let me pay when I invite you out to dinner," she told him as they exited the restaurant. His hand slid into the back pocket of her jeans once more. She tried to move away from him to walk around a large puddle, but he simply grabbed her by the waist and lifted her over.

He set her down on the other side then cupped her face with one hand. "It's sweet you want to pay your way, baby. But that's not the way things go in my world."

She frowned. "I have a job, Jed. It's not fair for you to have to pay whenever we go out. Not to mention you still haven't let me pay you back for those groceries you bought the other night."

"Firstly, the money you earn is yours."

Okay, now he was starting to really annoy her. Her money was hers then wasn't his money his?

"And when I take my girl out, no matter who invites who, I pay. I buy groceries or gas or anything else you need, then you don't pay me back. Especially if I'm eating said groceries. Maybe you call it old-fashioned, I call it being a man. Your man."

God, she liked the sound of that. She'd longed to be his again for so long. But still, she thought his views were wrong. She huffed out a breath. "I don't want to use you."

He stepped closer and kissed her forehead gently. "Baby girl, you're not using me."

"It feels like things are uneven."

He tucked her hair behind her ears. "You think there aren't things that you do for me that I can't reciprocate?"

She thought that through. "I can't think of any."

"Baby." He kissed her gently. But didn't say anything more.

She rolled her eyes. "You're gonna have to say more than baby for me to understand."

"You give me plenty. Your sweetness. Your smiles. And soon I'm gonna ask for more than that. But here isn't the place to discuss it."

She bit her lip to stop herself from asking him anything else. He was right, the parking lot wasn't a place to discuss things.

"Come on. It's getting late."

SHE FELT RIDICULOUSLY NERVOUS. What did he want to talk about? The drive home had been mostly silent, although he'd given her thigh a few reassuring squeezes.

"Don't worry. It's nothing dire. In fact, it might even be a relief for you to get this all out into the open," he told her as he walked with her up to her front door, his hand in the back pocket of her jeans once more.

That possessive gesture never failed to make her tummy go all gooey.

He grabbed her keys from her hand and unlocked the door himself. Once they were inside, their jackets stored away, she nervously found herself standing in the living room unsure what to do.

"Why don't you go get into your PJs, sweetheart," he suggested. "I'm going to check the windows and doors, make sure everything is secure."

She nodded and raced up the stairs.

"Slow down," he told her sternly. "You'll trip and hurt yourself."

Knowing he was right; she stopped her headlong run. She moved into her bedroom, wincing as she saw the mess in her room. She hurriedly stuffed clothes in drawers. Not that she thought tonight was going to lead to him in her bed.

But you never knew.

She searched through her drawers for some pajamas that weren't too childish. She finally settled on an oversized t-shirt and some cotton shorts. They would have to do. She quickly brushed her teeth, took off her make-up and moisturized. Then she wondered why she'd raced through her preparations because now she had nothing to do to put off this talk.

Damn it.

"Babe, you still getting ready or you hiding from me?"

Shit. Why did he have to be so smart?

"I'm coming," she called back.

She walked slowly down the stairs. He looked amused by the way she dragged her feet.

"We're just gonna chat. You're not about to be hung, drawn and quartered."

She blushed. "Sorry."

He reached out and grasped her around the waist, lifting her down the last few steps.

"Whose t-shirt is this, babe?" his voice was a soft, slightly unhappy rumble.

"This? Oh, it was Brad's."

"Not real keen on seeing you in another man's shirt, even your brother's."

"Oh. Right. Sorry." Guess she understood that. "I wouldn't like it if you wore another woman's shirt."

"I can guarantee that's not going to happen." The unhappiness was gone, his eyes filled with warmth.

Whoops. She hadn't meant to say that out loud.

Such a dork.

"Thought you might have worn a cute pair of pajamas like the other night."

She dropped her gaze. "I've had those for a while."

"Looked soft and comfy." He slid his arm around her waist. "Come on, let's talk. You need to get to bed soon."

"Uh, it's not yet ten. I usually stay up way later than this." He knew this, considering he'd called her before bed each night he couldn't be here.

"Not anymore," he said ominously.

What the heck did that mean?

JED DREW her into the living room. Ridiculously, he found himself nervous. Things had changed. This wasn't about working her out of his system. This was about something that had been between them for ten years. So he knew it was time to lay everything out on the table.

His girl needed his boundaries. Needed his discipline. Needed to know she was safe with him. So she could give him all of herself.

So, he set her on the sofa then sat his ass down on the coffee table so he could see her face. Leaning forward, he took her hands in his, wanting the connection.

"I'm starting to think I should be worried." Wide eyes studied him.

"Not worried, babe. Just want to get some things out there. You know I'm not big on you holding back from me."

She frowned slightly. "I haven't been."

"You have. I get it. But it's over now."

"Jed, I don't under—"

"You suck your thumb when you sleep."

She sucked in a breath. "Lots of people do that."

"You got a piece of blanket you cuddle with, rub it under your nose, it's part of one you had as a kid."

She tried to tug her hands back, but he held firm. "So?" There was a belligerent note to her voice but he knew it came from fear. She didn't have to be afraid.

"I think you're a Little. Pretty damn sure of it. What I don't know is if you know it."

"A Little?" she asked.

"You know I'm a dominant guy, I like control. Not just with sex. You get that, right?"

"Yeah, I've gotten that," she said cautiously.

"In the past I've gone to clubs, played with subs, never gotten serious with any of them."

"Do you mean BDSM clubs?"

"What do you know about BDSM clubs?" he demanded. Had she been to one before?

"I edit romance books, a couple of them had BDSM in them. So when you talk about me being a Little, do you mean age play?"

"Yeah, you edit any books about Littles?" He might need to read some of these books.

She shook her head. "No, I don't really know anything about it. You're really a Dom? You like bondage and spanking and stuff?" She blushed slightly.

"Yeah, I like doing that sort of stuff," he repeated, feeling the urge to smile. "I entered the scene when I was in the Navy. A friend introduced me to the scene. I've been around Littles. I like taking care of them, in all ways. But I've never met a Little who I wanted outside of a club scene. Until you."

"What about your fiancée?" she asked.

"Jennifer wasn't a submissive. She was the daughter of a friend of my grandfather. I was young. Didn't realize how ill-suited we were. We parted fairly amicably once we both realized we weren't what the other one wanted. How did you know about her anyway?"

She blushed bright red. "I. . .um. . .I looked you up. Found the engagement notice."

"Yeah. Her parents insisted on that. Don't see why have to announce that to everyone."

"She was never into that stuff?" she asked.

"No. Just one of the ways we weren't suited."

"You really think I'm a Little?"

"Yep."

"Because I suck my thumb and have a snuggly?"

"That's part of it. It's not just about what you do, though. It's who you are. And who I am. A Daddy Dom. I get this probably scares you, sugar. It's a lot. But it doesn't have to. My guess is you've suppressed that side of yourself for a long time. That you've been maybe embarrassed by it. But now you know you don't got to be. Not with me."

SHE LIKED when he called her sugar.

She was also scared shitless. The night he'd put her to bed, he'd obviously seen her suck her thumb, snuggle her bit of blankie. . .

And he hadn't left in disgust. He'd stuck around for days. More than that. He'd still shown her that he wanted her.

"You're not disgusted by it? By me acting like a child?"

"Told you that you could never embarrass me and I meant it. You certainly could never disgust me. You're sexy as hell. Those eyes, that hair, your gorgeous smile. And you're so sweet my teeth ache. This other part of you, hell, icing on the cake. I want it all, baby girl. I want you to give me your all."

Her mind whirled. "How does it all work? A Daddy Dom and a Little?"

"Works different for everyone. Just have to figure it out. For us, it means we no longer hide who we are. Means there might be times you're Little Daisy, other times you're adult Daisy. When you're in Little headspace, then I'm Daddy. I'm the man you come to for everything, protection, care, discipline. All the time. When you're Little, that will step up a notch. I'll give you baths, I'll give you playtime, corner time and spankings when they're needed. I'll give you a bedtime. A binky to replace your thumb. And I'll give you that safe haven you need to be you."

Her breath quickened. She really didn't know how she felt about all of this.

"What do I give you?"

He smiled. Her breath caught at the sight. "You give me you."

"That simple?" she asked.

"Wouldn't call it simple. Probably there will be hiccups along the way. But we work it out." He lifted her up onto his lap. "Together."

"I like the sound of that."

He leaned in and kissed her. "Thought you might." Then he stood, her cradled in his arms. "Time for bed."

"It's still early."

"Not for you. Now you have to be in bed by ten. Lights out by ten-thirty."

She stiffened as he climbed the stairs. "What? That's crazy!"

"Nope. It would be even earlier but I know you're a night-owl, so I'm easing you into it. Might make it even earlier if you keep arguing with me though," he warned.

She bit her lip and frowned.

"By the way, little girls who sulk generally find themselves over Daddy's knee before they're put to bed."

"I think I'm gonna be big Daisy tonight."

He shook his head with a grin. "Bedtime is for both of my girls."

"But I won't sleep."

"I got an idea to help with that." He walked into the bedroom and set her down on the bed. "Stay."

She resisted the urge to salute him. Just.

He just strode back to her, pajamas fisted in his huge, callused hand.

Then held out his hand to her. "Stand up, sugar."

She stood and he grabbed the bottom of her t-shirt. Her heart started to race. "Wh-what are you doing?"

"I like these jammies. Like you in them better than I like you in your brother's tee. So wear them for me, yeah?"

"O-okay," she said hesitantly. Fear slithered through her tummy. She took in a deep breath. She thought she was past this. It had been a long time. This was Jed. There was no reason for her to fear Jed.

"Calm, baby girl. Nothing's happening tonight, except for me giving you a reward for eating your salad. Arms up."

She raised her arms. She could do this. Would do this.

They weren't taking anything more from her. Not this.

He slid the t-shirt off and his gaze was caught on her breasts.

"Fuck me, you're beautiful."

Her tension eased slightly. "You've seen them before." They might not have had sex, but they had done plenty of playing.

"Oh yeah. Something a man doesn't forget but it's nothing like having them in front of you." She didn't breathe as he stared at her. Then he leaned down, circled her nipple with his tongue. Sucked it into his mouth.

Fuck. She swore she could feel that tug on her clit. She had to place her hands on his shoulders to hold herself steady. He lifted his head up, his eyes filled with heat. "Damn, baby."

Her thoughts exactly.

"You sure you couldn't rethink that whole no-sex thing tonight?" she asked. Heat was flooding her system, making it hard for her to think.

"Soon, baby. Real soon. Lie back on the bed."

Still in a fog of need, she climbed onto the bed and lay on her back. He undid her shorts and that haze started to clear.

"Jed."

"Hush," he told her. "No thinking. No worrying. All you got to do is lie back and let me take care of you."

She could do that. She thought. She raised her hips as he slid her shorts down. When he got them to her knees, he stilled, brought his hand to her still slightly bruised thigh. "How'd you do that, baby?"

"Bumped into something." She hated lying to him. It burned a hole in her gut and he wouldn't be happy if he knew.

She just had to make sure he never knew.

"Poor baby."

She was lucky he wasn't looking at her when she lied as she was pretty sure her poker face was crap. But he just kept pushing her shorts down her legs. He sat next to her, facing her, his thigh pressed against her side and took her in. He ran a finger lightly around each nipple then down her stomach to the top of her panties. They were satin, pale pink and had a small bow at the front.

"Pretty."

"I just bought them," she blurted out.

"For me?" his voice deepened.

"Yep."

"Like that even more."

She smiled at him. "Good," she whispered.

"Very good." He ran his finger along the top of her panties. "You don't sleep in panties anymore, though."

"I don't?"

"Nope. Don't sleep with pajama bottoms on either. When I'm in bed with you, I want to be able to get you without anything getting in my way."

Oh wow. Her heart raced so hard, she felt ill. "Bottom up, babe," he commanded.

She raised her ass and he slid the panties right off. Then his gaze turned to her. And locked on her pussy. He ran a finger over her bare lips.

"Shave this for me too?"

"Yes," she said so quietly it was a miracle he could hear.

"Like that too."

Thank God. She might not have had sex, but she knew things. And she figured most men liked a bare pussy. Still, she hadn't known what he would like.

"Spread your legs for me, babe."

Need rolled through her. Slowly, she pushed her thighs apart and let out a startled cry, reaching down to grab at his hand as he ran his finger around her swollen clit. He paused, gave her a stern look.

"Hands behind your head, baby girl."

"Wh-what?"

"Hands behind your head. Move them and I have another way of helping you sleep. Be much less pleasurable for you, though."

She quickly moved her hands.

"That's better. I want to touch my baby, then she's going to let me. You're so wet."

She knew. She could feel it. Did he like it, though? Then he brought his finger to his mouth, his finger that was coated in her dew and sucked it like it was the finest thing he'd ever tasted.

And so, she figured it was a good thing.

"My girl is going to stay nice and still while Daddy makes her come," he told her. "And she isn't going to hold anything back. Is she?"

She shook her head.

"Words, baby girl. Very important. I want communication open and clear between us at all times. Don't ever want to do something you don't enjoy. You say no, it means no and I stop. Understand?"

She nodded. Eyes wide. He waited.

Words, Daisy. You idiot.

"Yes."

"Yes, Daddy. Or Sir, if you're not ready for that. Dragon is acceptable when we're alone."

She grinned. Which she guessed was his intention.

"Good girl." He placed his finger on her clit, circling it slowly. Her hips rose, wanting more. "Keep still, baby girl. I want you to move, I tell you."

Her breath was coming faster, harder. "That's not that easy."

"Will get easier," he muttered, watching her closely. "Damn, my baby wants it bad, doesn't she? When was the last time you had an orgasm?"

"Last night," she told him. Then she froze as he did.

He moved his finger away. "What the fuck?"

"I-I gave myself one," she explained, looking away in embarrassment.

There was a moment of silence. Then his finger returned to her clit. But she was wound up too tight to pay much attention.

"What'd you think of as you made yourself come?" he asked as he lay on his side next to her. He grabbed the leg closest to him, lay it over his thighs, stretching her, widening her to his touch. He moved his finger away from her clit, ran it up and down her folds.

She wanted it back on her clit. Suddenly, he smacked his hand down lightly on her pussy. She let out a surprised cry.

"Daisy, asked a question. Not real keen on you not answering me."

Shit. Shit.

"You," she said quietly.

"Yeah?" he asked in a pleased voice. "I like that."

She blushed. Good Lord, were they really talking about her fantasies while she made herself come?

"But you don't do it again without me being here."

"What?" she squeaked. "I can't do that with you here."

"Oh, you can. You will." He leaned in, suckled on her nipple and played with her clit until she was so close, she could taste it. Until it pounded through her. Sweetness broke out in her mouth. She knew it was going to be good. So much better than anything she'd given herself.

Then he drew back. "Or if I'm on the phone with you. Yeah, that could work. If I can't be here to give you pleasure, I can direct you over the phone. Like that too."

Fucking hell. He was going to kill her.

He lightly pinched her clit and she jumped. "Hear me, Daisy-girl?" His voice was strict.

"Y-yes, Sir."

"That's my good girl. Now, my baby needs her sleep. Which means she needs to come for me. Nice and loud. Give it to me, baby girl."

He moved his finger faster, harder and she peaked. She threw her head back as her body shook with the force of the orgasm that hit her. It started slow and soft then it slammed into her, washing her away and she drifted.

From a distance she felt him shift. Felt his lips brush hers. Then her legs were spread even further and something warm and slightly rough applied to her lower lips. That's when she came back. She sat up, reaching for the washcloth, he was using to clean her up.

He sent her a look. "Where are your hands supposed to be, little girl?"

Oh. Crap. She moved them back.

"Your tally sure is getting large. Might have to spread it out so you can still sit to work. Or get you one of those standing desks. Yeah, that might be a better idea."

He stood, returned the wash cloth to the bathroom. No throwing it on the floor for Jed. She lay there until he walked back. Guilt filled her. She should do something for him. This felt one-sided. He sat and picked up the nightie he'd dropped.

"Sit up, baby girl. Let's get you ready for bed."

"Um, isn't there something you'd like me to do for you?" she asked shyly. She had zero experience with giving a blow job, but she was willing to learn. Very willing.

"Not right now, sugar. Although I appreciate the offer. But I want my first time with you in your pussy and I got to work you up to taking my cock."

Probably more than he even realized. She pushed that thought back. That was for another day. She yawned as he pulled her nightie on then picked her up and stood her by the bed.

"You need to go potty, sugar?"

She stared at him in horror. Did he just ask her that?

"What?"

"Do you need to go potty?"

"I. . .ah. . ."

He gave her a knowing look. "Take it that's a yes. Come on."

"Well. . .this is more than a little embarrassing."

He stopped at the door to the bathroom and drew her close. "Sugar, ain't nothing that you and I can't talk about. No need to be embarrassed. I'll even let you go by yourself. This time."

This time?

She gawked at him for a moment. He turned her towards the door and gave her a gentle push. "Off you go."

Somehow her body rallied and she stumbled into the bathroom, firmly shutting the door because. . .yikes, she wasn't ready for that. Wasn't sure she ever would be. Then she did her business and wandered back out in a sleepy stupor.

"You wash your hands?"

"Yes," she whispered, knowing her face was once more an unappealing shade of crimson.

"Good girl. Come on, in you go." He'd already pulled back the covers.

When she was in the bed, he tucked her in tight he reached over and grabbed blankie, giving it to her. She studied his face, looking for any signs he thought her a complete freak. But all she saw was reassurance and acceptance. "Gonna sleep well now, baby girl?"

"Uh-huh," she murmured, her eyes already closing, her thumb slipping into her mouth automatically.

"Good," he told her. "Happy dreams, sugar."

"Hi," she said breathlessly into the phone.

"Hello, sugar." His voice rolled over her, instantly filling her with happiness. "Where are you?"

"Just walking up to the house. I went to the grocery store." She'd only needed a few things and decided that wasn't worth doing an online order for.

"Call me back once you're inside and groceries are put away." He ended the call before she could answer. As she walked up to the front door, a weird feeling assaulted her. Like someone was watching her.

Don't be silly.

Once inside, she locked the door and hurriedly put the few things in her shopping bag away before calling Jed back.

"Sugar."

Because of his schedule, she hadn't seen him since that night he'd given her an orgasm and tucked her into bed, but they'd talked a lot. He'd put her to bed each night over the phone.

It was easier than she'd thought to relax and be herself around him. She guessed he was right. All she'd needed was a place where she knew she was secure, and out her Little side came.

"Hi."

"Groceries away?"

"Yep."

"Good girl." Those words still filled her with warmth. "Got good news. Working late tonight, but then I've got the next two days off."

Excitement filled her. And a hint of nerves.

"Gonna pack a bag and come stay. If that's okay with you." There was a note of hesitation in his voice. Her nerves melted.

"I would love that," she said quietly.

"Good. Me too. Remember, nothing happens you don't want, but while I'm there I want to be in your bed, holding you. Been dreaming of that for a while now."

Her breath hitched. "Me too."

"You up to date on your work? Can you take some time off?"

"Yep." If she got her butt into gear now.

"Good. Because also been thinking we need to start getting through that tally you've managed to accumulate."

Her mouth dropped open. "I don't think that's necessary."

"Got to do it some time, baby girl."

"But I don't want to," she said with a pout.

"Not about what you want, is it? It's about what you need."

"I don't need a spanking." She stomped her foot. Then she looked at it in surprise. Where the hell had that come from?

"And I would say I've waited too long to give you what you need. Now, I can tell that someone didn't get enough sleep last night, am I right?"

Maybe.

"Little girl. . ."

"I woke up at three and couldn't sleep," she admitted.

"Early to bed for you tonight."

"Nooo," she groaned.

"Yes," he said firmly. "Keep arguing and you'll be spending the next fifteen minutes in the corner with your pants down at your feet."

That she did not want.

"Sorry, Sir," she whispered.

"That's better. Baby, I know you're probably nervous. Unsure about all this. But I'm gonna keep you safe, you know that right?"

Warmth filled her. "Yes, I know."

"Nothing bad happens to my girl while Daddy is around, right?"

"Yes. I'm sorry."

"Go get what work you need to finish up done. I'll call you at eight to put you to bed."

Eight! Man, that sucked.

She knew better than to say that out loud, though.

THE DOORBELL RANG EARLY the next morning and she raced to it, checking briefly to make sure it was him. Something she hadn't forgotten to do since his warning. Then she opened the door, and unable to help herself, she launched herself at him.

Thankfully, he'd seemed to read her intent because he braced himself and caught her. His hands on her ass as she wrapped herself around him and held on tight.

"Hey there, sugar."

She could read the amusement in his voice. She didn't care if he thought she was a dork. But then he stepped forward, through the door shutting it behind him. And then she was on her feet and he was kissing her.

A kiss that was so hot, she thought she was melting. In fact, she was shocked to find she could still stand when he drew back.

"Think my baby missed me," he rumbled before reaching over to lock the door.

"Yeah," she said breathlessly. Then she just stared at him for a moment, feeling shy for some reason.

He reached out and cupped the side of her face. "Missed you too, babe."

She gave him a smile.

"How is my Daisy-girl?" he asked.

"Good."

"Got a present for you," he told her. And for the first time, she noticed the dark green duffel over his shoulder.

"A present?" Excitement filled her. "Really?"

"Yep." He tilted his head to one side, a slight smile on his face.

She clapped her hands as she bounced on her feet. "Yay! Oh, but I didn't get you anything."

He shook his head. "Not why I bought you it, babe. I bought you a few things. Might not like all of them, though."

What did that mean?

"I'd like any gift you bought me," she told him as he slid his hand into the back pocket of her jeans. Normally, she wore yoga pants when she was home doing nothing. But since he seemed to like to rest his hand on her ass, she'd put a pair of jeans on this morning. "I don't remember the last time anyone bought me anything."

He glanced down at her and she couldn't read his face. They reached the living room but instead of sitting on the couch as she'd expected, he sat down on the rug on the floor. So, she sat across from him. He opened the duffel bag and pulled out a large box that was wrapped in pretty unicorn paper.

"Got the paper from Ellie," he told her in a rough voice. "Ordered it online."

She held the large box in her hand. Something shifted around inside it. Excitement filled her. "Can I open it?"

"Sure can, sugar."

She tore at the paper and he let out a surprised bark of laughter that had her stilling and looking at him.

"What?" he asked.

"Nothing. I just. . .I haven't heard you laugh in a long time. I like it."

His eyes warmed. "Like hearing you laugh too."

She pulled the rest of the paper away. And stared down at what she held in her hands.

"You said you liked building blocks; thought you might like this. But if you don't—"

She launched herself at him again. Only this time, he wasn't expecting it and he hadn't braced. So, she caught him off guard and he went flying back. She lay on top of him, pressing kisses over his face until, laughing, he sat up and pulled her onto his lap.

He grinned down at her. "I'm guessing you like it."

"I love it." She bounced around. "Can I open it now?"

"In a minute. I'll even help you build it."

"You will?" She stared up at him in wonder. "You'll play with me?"

"Of course, what is a daddy for if he won't play with his girl?"

Her happiness washed away the last of her doubts about him accepting this. He'd listened to her when she'd told him she liked to relax by building things. He'd gone online and bought her the most kickass Lego set she'd ever seen, a princess castle complete with horses, knights, a moat and best of all. . .dragons. Then he'd gone to Ellie to get unicorn wrapping paper. And now he was going to help her build it.

She reached up and lightly pressed her lips against his. "Thank you, Daddy." God that felt good to finally call him that. "Best present ever."

And then he topped that gift by giving her an even better one.

His eyes melted into pools of hazel-green and the widest smile filled his face. He hugged her tight. "You're welcome."

His voice was slightly husky. But she got it. This moment was special. It was the moment she truly gave him her Little to protect.

"Before you open it, baby girl, let me get the rest of your presents."

"Don't think anything could be better than this, Daddy," she told him solemnly.

He set her back on the floor then reached back into his bag. Next thing he drew out wasn't wrapped. She stared down at the binky in his hand. It looked far bigger than anything she'd ever seen a baby use.

"I'm not a baby," she told him instantly.

"I want you to use this instead of sucking on your thumb. It's an orthodontic one."

She scowled. "What's wrong with my thumb?"

"This is better for your teeth."

"I'll probably lose it." And maybe that would be on purpose.

He raised one eyebrow. "I thought I could tie it to your snuggly so you wouldn't lose it."

Damn it. He knew she would never lose her snuggly. She let out a disgruntled sigh.

He rubbed her knee gently. "Give it a try, huh? For me? Don't want you messing up your teeth."

Her tummy bubbled with happiness. "All right, I'll try."

"That's my good girl." He reached into his bag again, brought out some Winnie-the-Pooh coloring-in books, story books and, best of all, three nighties. One with Tigger, one with Eeyore and one with Kanga and Roo.

She picked them up with a squeal. "These. Are. Awesome!"

He grinned. "Saw them. Thought of you."

"Thank you, Daddy! Can't wait to wear them!"

"That's good. You can try them out when you take a nap later."

That killed her good mood. "Nope, don't need a nap."

"You look tired, despite going to bed early last night."

"I woke up early," she told him.

"Half a mind to put you back to bed now, but I thought you'd want to play with your Legos."

Damn him. She did want to play and she definitely didn't want to go for a nap now.

"Last gift. Doubt you'll see it as such, though." He drew out a small, flat wooden paddle.

She froze. "What's that for?"

"This is Daisy's naughty girl paddle."

She shook her head. "No, it's not."

"Yes, it is."

"Nope." She shook her head so hard, her hair whipped around her face.

"Baby girl," he said in a warning voice.

"Daisy doesn't need a naughty girl paddle," she said, her voice growing more childish. She watched his face grow soft, but didn't take much notice since she was too busy denying the existence of the paddle in his hand. Ouch. How much would that hurt?

She couldn't even imagine.

"Daisy is a good girl," she insisted.

He nodded, surprising her. "Daisy is a good girl. But sometimes she does naughty things. And sometimes, she will get the paddle on her bare bottom to help her remember to obey the rules she has to follow."

She folded her arms over her chest. "Daisy doesn't want it. Give it to another naughty girl."

This time when he smiled, it stuck. And it was beautiful. And for a moment she forgot about that stinking paddle and just stared at him.

Then he turned it. "But it has Daisy's name on it."

And yes, it did. In flowing script. Right along the handle.

"You had it engraved?" she yelled.

"Yep," he replied. "Now, just got to find a good place to put it."

"The fireplace?" she asked hopefully.

He gave her a stern look. "Nope. And if it ends up in there, I won't be happy. I also ordered a back-up for my cabin at the ranch."

Did that mean he was going to invite her out there one day? So far, they'd spent all their time at her place. Not that she minded, she loved this house.

"I think we'll put it up on the mantel for the moment," he told her. "Might end up hanging it somewhere once I figure out the best place for it."

Hmm, she wasn't sure she wanted that thing hanging in her house. She sent the paddle a dirty look.

She'd find that paddle a nice home. In the garbage.

Then Jed turned back and she dropped her face to the Legos with a smile. Hey, she had an awesome present and her daddy was here.

Death of the paddle could wait for another day.

"Sugar? Where are you? You playing hide and seek or something?" Jed called out.

And something. Shit. She frantically chewed on the mouthful of gummy bears, knowing she was gonna be in trouble if he found her before she was done. Didn't really dawn on her to spit it out. She was totally in Little headspace. She raced towards the large sideboard that ran along one wall of the dining room and managed to squeeze herself between it and the wall as she chewed.

"All right, little girl. I want you to show yourself right now."

Uh-oh, that was his strict voice. He wasn't playing around now. Why had she put so many gummies in her mouth at once?

Amateur move. She'd gotten so excited when she found where he'd hidden them, that she'd grabbed a whole lot at once. Then when she heard him calling for her, she'd panicked and shoved them in her mouth.

And now she was in deep trouble. Because Daddy didn't want her eating any sweets that he hadn't given her. Which is why he'd hidden all of hers.

"Gonna count to three, and you don't want me to get to three."

Her bottom cheeks clenched together at that threat.

"One."

Uh-oh.

"Two!" Jed called out. Shit!

She stepped out, placing both hands over her mouth as if she thought that meant he wouldn't notice she was chewing frantically.

He walked over to her. "What's in your mouth, little girl?"

She shook her head. She couldn't talk right now.

"Spit it out." He held up his hand to her mouth.

Her eyes widened. He didn't seriously think she was going to spit the mess in her mouth into his hand?

"Out. Now."

Okay, he meant business. She pointed at the kitchen. He just shook his head. And feeling completely embarrassed, she opened her mouth and spat out the sticky mess. Gross.

"Gummy bears?" he asked calmly.

She nodded.

"What is Daddy's rule about candy and chocolate?"

"I've got to ask you if I want some," she said.

"That's right," he said sternly. "Now, I'm gonna go clean up this mess and you're gonna take your pants and panties off and then go stand facing the corner."

"What? No," she whined.

He raised an eyebrow. "What was that?"

"Nothing, Daddy."

She grabbed at her jeans and pulled them down.

"Panties too," he said sternly.

She dragged them down over her bottom. Damn, this was embarrassing. She bent to pull them off her feet.

"Keep them around your ankles," he stopped her. "Corner. Now."

She shuffled over, grumbling to herself. She couldn't take a full step so it took her twice as long to get to the free corner in the living room.

"Nose touching the wall," he called from the kitchen.

She did not like this.

"Someone is in dire need of a good spanking and a nap," he commented, sounding closer.

"No," she groaned.

"I think daily naps are going to become a regular thing for you."

What kind of crap was that?

"Just as well you have a job where you can be flexible with your hours."

She pouted at that. Then she stomped her foot. "I'm not having a nap."

"Oh yes, you are, little one. Right after your spanking." He took a gentle hold of her wrist and turned her. Then he led her out of the corner to the chair he'd pulled away from the dining room table.

Uh-oh. Maybe stomping her foot and giving him sass hadn't been in her best interests.

"Um, Daddy, shouldn't we finish the Lego castle?" she said hopefully.

"It will still be there later."

"Well, maybe I should go have that nap now. I'm kind of tired."
She yawned as he sat in the chair and stared up at her.

"Nap after. Spanking first."

Biting her lip, she lay herself over his lap.

"You want me to hold your hands for you?" he asked in a gruff
voice.

Considering this was her first spanking, she had no idea.

"I-I don't k-know." She was starting to tremble in a mix of
shock and trepidation.

"Baby, you're shaking," he said in a surprisingly tender voice.
He laid his hand on her bottom but not to spank it, rather to rub
soothing circles along her full cheeks. "Scared?"

"A little."

"It's all right to be a bit nervous. Shouldn't have left it so long
to do this, but I wanted you to know me again. To trust me. But
you've probably built this up as scarier than it really is. It's just a
spanking. I know I'm a big guy, but I've given these in the past. I
know what I'm doing."

She really didn't want to hear about any spankings he'd given
in the past.

"I don't know your pain tolerance, though. This is your first
spanking so I'm going to take care with you. I would never want to
harm you. I would never want to scare you. You being nervous is
fine. Frightened is not. You know the sort of relationship I want.
Who I am. But if you ever decide you don't want this then ulti-
mately you have all the power. I'm not taking your submission.
You give it to me."

She thought through all of that. She liked that. That he wasn't
taking anything. On the other hand, that meant she was giving
him permission to take charge and spank her.

But the truth was, she felt better with the boundaries he'd laid
down. For the first time in a long time, she didn't feel like a weirdo.

And the voice telling her that she was worthless and white trash had disappeared down to a whisper.

Because of Jed. Because he accepted her for who she was. And part of who she was needed to know he would follow up on his word.

So, she took a deep breath and relaxed.

"You accepting my dominance, baby girl?" he asked her, still rubbing her ass. Damn, she quite liked that.

"Yes, Daddy."

"And everything that comes with that?"

"Yes, Daddy."

"That's my good girl. Now, I'm gonna give you a safe word. You can use it if things ever go too far, if you ever become scared but it's not a get-out-of-a-spanking free card," he warned. "And I got more punishments I can use. Understand?"

"Yes, Daddy."

"Your safe word is fruit. Understand?"

"Yes. I understand."

Without another word, he laid a sharp slap on her ass. And holy shit! That hurt.

Another smack landed before she could protest. He wasn't messing around. These were hard, and fast. Soon her ass was stinging, heat invading deep and she found her breath coming in sharp gasps. And she didn't know what the hell to do with her hands. She couldn't touch the floor. They were just hanging there. So, she grasped hold of his calf and held on for dear life.

"No, it's enough!" she cried out.

"Oh, baby, we're not there yet." There was sympathy in his voice. And determination.

That did not bode well for her.

Smack! Smack! Smack!

Why had she eaten the candy? She had to have known she'd be caught, right? Jed didn't miss much.

Which meant she'd probably wanted to get caught? That she'd wanted this?

No. That was crazy talk.

"Time to learn when Daddy gives you a rule, you're to listen and obey." Smack, smack, smack. "I'm not doing it to be mean. You can still have your candy." Slap, slap, slap. "But not so much that it puts holes in your teeth and gives you diabetes. Understand?"

He paused. And she sobbed, trying to catch her breath, knowing he was waiting for a reply.

"I-I understand."

"Good. I'm going to carry on, and give you the thirty you've accumulated."

"No," she cried out, kicking her feet.

"Believe me, baby. You won't feel like waiting until later for these."

He placed his hand on the small of her back. Then his hand landed again and she screeched, certain she couldn't take another thirty. But she didn't say her safe word. She'd earned these. She knew the consequences. And he wouldn't ever harm her.

Tears dripped down her face, falling on the floor. They poured out of her. She let out a deep sob, this one less about the pain of the spanking and more about the ache that lived inside her. A dam broke, tears poured and she felt the tight lid she kept on her most agonizing memories start to loosen.

She barely noticed him stopping, was too caught up in the rush of emotion filling her. Then draining away. Her breath hitched and sobbed. Jed turned her in his arms and carried her through the living room and upstairs to her bedroom. He murmured to her soothingly the entire way. She didn't pay as much attention to the words as she did the tone, which was loving and sweet.

He laid her on the bed then lay beside her, gathering her close. She half-lay over his chest and cried. He ran his hand up and down her back and let her. He didn't try to make her stop or get her to talk. He just let her be. Gradually, the tears disappeared. The sobs died down. She was left feeling drained. Her insides were empty. For the first time in years the pain wasn't there.

She was under no illusion that it was anything other than a temporary fix. But it felt amazing.

She also had a throbbing head, was thirsty as hell and her butt hurt.

"My butt's sore," she commented, lifting her head.

He rolled them so she was on her side. His gaze stared down at her as he leaned up on one elbow.

"That was a lot of tears, baby," he commented cautiously. Probably worried he was about to set her off again.

Poor guy.

"I know. Sorry."

"More tears than I figure that spanking warranted since I was pretty easy on you."

Her mouth dropped open. "That was easy?"

His lips twitched. "Guess it's safe to say you don't have the highest pain tolerance."

She nodded solemnly. "I don't think you should ever spank me again."

He tweaked her nose. "All you got to do in order to avoid a punishment spanking is follow the rules, little one."

She sighed. "I'm doomed then."

He let out a chuckle and she smiled.

He sobered up. "Wanna tell me what was going on in that head of yours?"

She shrugged. "I just. . .I don't know. I started to cry from the spanking and then I was crying for other reasons."

He stiffened slightly. "Anything I can do about those other reasons?"

Not unless he wanted to reopen the past. "No, I don't think so.

It was just stuff about my family. About the past. Stuff I guess I buried deep and haven't dealt with."

He was silent, thinking. She didn't think that was good. "You know, I'm thinking you should cut down on your workouts."

"What?" He gave her a startled look.

"Yeah, you're a bit too muscly now. I like a bit of flab on my guys. Especially their arms. Be good if your arms weren't very strong."

He rolled his eyes. "Baby, I wasn't using my full strength."

"Felt like it." She wrinkled her nose.

He kissed the tip of her nose. "Like I said, sugar, don't like the spanking, don't break the rules."

Easier said than done.

"Now, I gotta go find a new hiding place for the candy and you're going to have a nap."

"Noooo, I don't need a nap," she cried.

"Sugar, you're completely exhausted."

"We haven't finished the castle."

"We can finish it later. Got to take care of my girl, and right now she needs sleep. Now, do you need to go potty?"

A blush filled her cheeks. "No."

"All right. I'm gonna get you something to wear." He climbed up and she sighed. Although she'd meant it to sound disgruntled, it became something dreamier as she watched that ass of his in those just-right jeans.

Damn.

Her pussy clenched. Maybe she should ask him to help her to get to sleep. He came back with one of her new nighties in his hand. The Eeyore one.

She loved Eeyore.

"Sit up, baby."

She scowled up at him. "I don't think sitting is an option. Don't think I'll be sitting comfortably for a long time."

He rolled his eyes. "Wasn't that hard, sugar. And think on the positive side, now your slate is wiped clean. And our time together is free and clear."

Heat filled his gaze and she found herself staring at his lips, wondering if he was going to kiss her.

"On your knees, let's get you to bed for a nap."

"I'm really not tired." She tried to communicate with her gaze what she really wanted.

He raised an eyebrow then picked her up and set her on her feet on the side of the bed. Then he leaned down and kissed her, a light peck that wasn't anything close to what she wanted. He whipped off her t-shirt then drew off her bra.

"Won't be needing this for a while," he muttered.

"I won't?"

"Nope."

"What if we go out somewhere?"

"We're not going out anywhere," he told her.

"What if we run out of food?" she challenged.

"Then we get some take-out delivered."

"What if we run out of toilet paper?"

"You need more toilet paper?"

"No," she admitted. "I got some just yesterday. But what if—"

"Baby, there any real reason you can't go without wearing a bra for rest of the day? It uncomfortable for you? Make your breasts hurt? Cause you back problems?"

"No."

"Then do this for me, yeah? The nightie, that's for you. No bra and no panties, that's for me."

"No panties?"

"Yeah, like the idea of you in a short nightie or dress with nothing on underneath."

"Oh. Okay," she agreed.

He gave her another kiss. This one not light. Or quick. By the time he finished, she was breathing heavily and swaying where she stood. He managed to pull her nightie over her head without much help from her.

Then he pulled back the covers. "Climb into bed, sugar. Time for a nap."

"But..."

"No big girl time after a spanking," he told her.

"Well, that sucks," she muttered as she climbed into bed and rolled onto her side. He surprised her by placing one pillow on the mattress behind her. Then he grabbed another one and positioned it in front of her.

"What are you doing?" she asked.

"Making sure you don't roll out of bed."

Oh. That was slightly odd. And yet so protective it felt nice.

"But with you just wearing a nightie for the rest of the day, no bra, no panties, big girl play is bound to come later."

She liked the sound of that. A lot.

He tucked the blanket around her. Reaching over he grabbed that damn binky off her nightstand.

She frowned. Especially when she noticed he'd secured it to her snuggly. Not sure how she felt about that.

"Give it a go, sugar," he told her in a gentle voice. "For me."

Damn it. He had to know she couldn't resist when he asked her to do things for him in that voice. She nodded and he gave her those warm eyes in return.

Totally worth it.

"Open."

He slid the binky into her mouth and she sucked on it experimentally. Tasted a bit funny. She really wasn't sure about it. At all.

"Give it time, sugar." He leaned in and kissed her forehead. "Cute as a button."

She let out a happy sigh as he ran his fingers through her hair then down her neck. She leaned over the pillow in front of her so he could reach her tight muscles. She yawned.

Then she drifted off to sleep.

HE HAD her nicely tucked up on his lap, her ass wiggled against his cock making him groan. He kissed her again, cupping her breast, he ran his thumb over the tight nub. She let out a whimpering noise.

Fuck, yes.

He didn't know how he'd managed to function these few weeks, his balls were aching, his mind constantly filled with thoughts of her naked and under him, of her riding him, of her spread-eagled and tied to his bed while he ate her out.

Yeah, he had fucking blue balls.

Tonight, he was determined to taste her. He was going to settle himself between those thighs and eat until he was sated. Might take a while.

He was a man with a big appetite. And he was pretty certain she was gonna become his favorite treat.

This afternoon, she'd woken from her nap and come to find him while she was still half-asleep, her hair all tousled and her eyes heavy-lidded. Each time she'd raised her hand to wipe at her eyes, that too-short nightie had ridden up giving him a glimpse of her red bottom or that gorgeous fucking pussy, depending on which way she was facing.

Adorable.

He'd discovered that after she napped, it took her a while to fully wake up and he hadn't been happy she'd walked down the stairs in that condition. So she had a new rule that she had to call out for him to come get her when she woke up. She hadn't been happy. That's when he'd had her turn around and lift her nightie up over her hips so he could check on how red she still was. By the time he was finished inspecting her, her face was a much brighter red than her butt and he was so hard he was aching.

While she was napping, he'd taken the opportunity to do a bit more online shopping. He'd gotten himself a camera monitor for when she was napping.

He'd also taken a look at beds. Something that might resemble a cot without actually being one. He'd found this gorgeous wooden bed that was painted white with three solid sides that curled at the top. A sleigh daybed was the description. Which was perfect since he didn't want her sleeping separate from him during the night. But when she was having a nap, he liked the idea of her sleeping in a cot-like bed.

But Little time was over now. It was time for some big girl play. He drew his head away from where he'd been kissing her neck and looked down at her.

"Babe, look at me."

"Don't stop."

"Daisy-girl. Look at me." He injected more steel into his voice and she looked up at him immediately. Fucked if he didn't love that. "I want to know if this is moving too fast?"

"Too fast?" she groaned. Then she rolled her hips against his dick. Fuck him.

Fuck him.

He grabbed her hips, holding her still. "Daisy, you sure?"

"I'm sure," she said breathlessly.

He pulled her mouth to his. Ravaged it. Damn she could kiss. This time she was the one to pull back.

"Got to tell you something first, though." She sounded hesitant, unsure. He tensed. But before he could reply, his phone rang. Shit. Fuck. He gave her an apologetic look. "I'm so sorry, sugar. That's my work ringtone. I have to get it."

Her eyes looked glazed and she blinked up at him then shook her head as though shaking it free of cobwebs. "That's okay."

He set her aside then snatched up the phone. "Yeah?"

"Sorry to bother you, man," Corbin said to him. "Tracking job has come up and they need you. Two kids have been taken. The police think it's their father. Parents are estranged. Mother wants to hire us to help find them."

Kids. Fuck. He hated when it was kids. "I'll be there soon as I can."

"Roger that."

He ended the call and turned to Daisy. "Baby, I'm sorry."

Christ, he hated leaving her. "You have to go, it's all right."

"If it wasn't important, I wouldn't."

"I understand. Really."

"Some kids have gone missing. They need my help finding them." He didn't know why he told her. He wasn't supposed to talk about the job, but he needed her to know he wouldn't leave her without good reason.

Her whole face softened and she clasped her hands together. "Kids? Someone has kidnapped children? Oh my God that's terrible. Go. Go. Don't worry about me."

But he did worry about her. That was the thing.

"I don't know how long I'm gonna be gone." He clasped her face between his hands. "I want you to remember your rules. I still want you to text me before you go to bed. I may not be able to call you but I'll see your text, and return it when I can. And I'll be noting what time it is. Same goes with your food. I want photos of what you're eating."

"Jed, you don't need to be thinking about any of this while you're trying to find those kids. I can take care of myself."

"You're right about me needing to focus. Which means I can't check in as often as I'd like. Doesn't mean I don't want to know how you're doing when I got a chance, all right?"

"All right, honey."

First time she'd called him that. He liked it.

"You need anything. Anything at all. You call the boys."

"The boys?"

"The guys I work with at JSI." He'd explained to her what JSI was and what his job entailed. She thought it sounded exciting and a bit scary. "I'll put the number in your phone if you get it for me."

She nodded, looking around with a frown. "Where did I put that thing?"

"You find your phone while I pack up, yeah?"

When he got back downstairs, his duffel over his shoulder, she was waiting in the foyer, her hand clutching her phone. She handed over her phone to him. He put in JSI's main line, which was manned 24/7.

"You can call them anytime, day or night. I should have introduced you to them so you knew them, but I've let them know you're under my protection. I'll call you if I can, but—"

"It's okay, I understand. Please don't worry about me. I'll be fine. You find those children. And be careful."

"So sweet." He kissed her forehead. "I want to hear the door lock behind me."

She rolled her eyes. Brat. "I always lock the door behind you."

"Good. See that never changes. Damn sorry I didn't get to taste you tonight."

She was blushing bright red as she looked up at him. "Me too."

He let out a surprised bark of laughter and her blush grew deeper. "You're good for me, sugar. Forgot what it was like to laugh."

"I'll make sure you don't ever forget again."

11

Daisy heard something at the front door and jumped up, her heart racing. Two days had passed since Jed left and other than a brief text message last night, she hadn't heard from him. She hoped he was all right. She was barely able to sleep from worrying about him and those kidnapped kids. And since he wasn't around to make her, she wasn't taking any naps so she was tired and jumpy.

She'd thought about calling Jed's 'boys'. But it seemed silly to call just to see if they'd heard from him. They had important jobs; they didn't need her bothering them because she was worried about her . . .whatever he was.

Although maybe she should call them about all the odd phone calls she'd been getting. But nothing had happened except for a few weird hang-ups she didn't feel it was worth bothering them.

She ran towards the door, remembering to check first to see who was on the other side. When she glanced out the window, no one was there.

She unlocked her door and opened it, staring down at the bunch of flowers in surprise. They didn't look like the sort that a florist created. These had been freshly picked, and bunched together without any real thought. They were still beautiful, though. And it was a thoughtful gesture.

Who were they from? Not Jed. Even if he was home, it wouldn't be something he would do anyway. He would knock on the door and hand them to her. Then invite himself in. Then start bossing her around. Checking she was getting enough sleep and that she hadn't found the stash of candy, which she'd upended the house looking for so she had no idea where he'd put it.

The bastard.

Warmth burst through her at the thought of how he cared for her. She looked more closely at the flowers which were tied at the stems with a rubber band. No note.

Oh well, she wasn't going to turn them down. She loved flowers. She took another look around, though. Maybe it was just someone in the neighborhood being friendly. She locked the door then found a vase in the kitchen and half-filled it with water then put it on the windowsill.

JED FROWNED as the phone rang and rang. Where was she? He paced back and forth. Maybe she was out somewhere and couldn't hear the phone.

Except she wasn't big on going out. She was a homebody.

Perhaps she was in the shower. Or maybe someone had broken into her house and hurt her or she'd slipped and hit her head or. . . the list kept growing in his head. If she didn't answer this time then he was going to get one of the boys to go around and check on her.

"Hello? Jed?" her voice sounded breathless.

"Daisy? Everything all right?" His voice was curt.

"Yes, of course. I was just upstairs and my phone was downstairs. Are you all right? What's going on? Have you found the kids?"

He sighed. "Not yet. I'm just calling 'cause it's probably going to be a few more days and I didn't want you to worry."

"Oh, I'm so sorry," she told him.

"I know, baby. Me too." Christ he was tired. "What you up to?"

"I was just going to have a shower."

"Yeah? You naked already?"

"What? No!"

"That's disappointing."

"Is this. . ." her voice lowered. "Is this a sex call?"

He threw back his head and laughed. "What?"

"Well. . .you know. . .when people have sex over the phone."

"Baby girl, we haven't even had sex for real."

"I know, but you asked me if I was naked."

And now he had the picture of her naked body in his mind. He felt himself harden. Damn, he wished he was home with her.

"Jed? You still there? Everything all right?"

"Yeah, baby. Just tired and missing you."

"Miss you too."

"Everything all good there?"

"Yep."

"You eating good? No sugar?"

"No sugar." There was a definite pout in her voice. "But I've got to get some for Halloween soon."

"Still six weeks away, baby. Stores aren't gonna run out of candy before I get home. Besides, that stash you've got would be enough to last three Halloweens so don't expect we'll have to get more."

She gave a disgruntled sigh. He had to grin. Cute.

"Sure you're okay?" he asked again.

"Yes. Everything is fine here."

Something sounded off to him. "You sure about that?"

"Yep. I'm boring. Nothing interesting ever happens to me."

DAISY WINCED AFTER SAYING THAT. Why point that out to him? He probably knew but she didn't have to say it. He was Mr. Tough Guy extraordinaire, he jetted around the world to save the day. And she was Miss Boring Pants who preferred staying in and watching movies and eating her weight in junk food.

"I like the life you have. Nothing I like more after a stressful day than coming home to you. Sometimes it's what gets me through the day, thinking about sitting on your couch with you curled up around me, some stupid reality TV show on that I don't understand, but sure as shit enjoy watching you enjoying it. Right now, I'd pay anything to be there with you."

She smiled. "I'm glad I can give that to you."

"Me too, baby. Me too."

He sounded exhausted and she hated that. "I need to get back to work." He yawned.

"And maybe get some sleep," she added, tickled that the shoe got to be on the other foot.

"How much sleep did you get last night, sugar?"

Drat. That backfired.

"Probably more than you."

He snorted. "I damn well hope so. You caught up on your work?"

"Pretty much, yeah."

"Good. Then I want you to go have a healthy dinner. Then take a nice long bubble bath. Shave everything and I do mean every-thing," his voice went lower and she gulped. "Climb into one of your nighties and I want you in bed by nine."

"No!"

"Yep, nine. I want you well rested for when I get home.

Although I might have to sleep for twenty-four hours straight before I'm capable of doing anything."

Softness filled her. "All right, I'll go to bed early."

"Good girl. Remember call the boys if you need them."

"I wouldn't want to be a bother." Unease filled her. She knew she should tell him about the flowers, but he had so much going on.

"You could never be a bother."

Oh. That was nice.

"I've got to go, baby girl."

"Okay, stay safe."

"Always. Got a good reason to now, don't I?"

She ended the call, a ridiculous smile on her face.

Got a good reason to now, don't I?

She did a twirl. This was everything she'd ever wanted. Jed. Wanting her. Caring about her. Her gaze landed on the flowers and she came to a shuddering halt. She bit her lip. Who could they be from? Could still be a neighbor. Although why no note? Why not wait to talk to her?

You should have told Jed.

It was one bunch of flowers. It didn't mean anything.

12

She felt ill.

Daisy paced back and forth and stared at the three bunches of flowers. Three! What was happening here? Who was sending them?

She rubbed at her stomach. She had barely slept in days. Or eaten. She was so stressed she couldn't even work. She hadn't left the house in days. Not unusual for her, but rather than it being because she didn't want to, it was because she was too scared to.

The first bunch of flowers she'd thought were sweet. The bunch the next day made her feel uneasy. The bunch on the third day had her rattled. Then last night before she went to bed, she'd found a note. Words typed on a piece of plain white paper. Nothing distinguishing about it. But it was the creepiest thing she'd ever read.

DAISY.

I see you. Staying inside your house will not stop me. I particularly like watching you undress. It's so hot. You need some sexier lingerie though. Get something slinky and tight. Something I'll want to fuck you in.

Always watching.

VOMIT ROSE in her throat and she raced towards the toilet. She tasted bile right before she threw up. It didn't stop. It kept coming even though there was nothing left in her stomach. And crap it hurt.

There was a knock on the door and she jumped with a scream. It took her a few seconds to calm her racing heart. Whoever was doing this wouldn't knock, she reassured herself. Still, she was shaking as she flushed the toilet and splashed water on her face.

She was all right. Everything was okay. It was way past time to call Jed's boys though. She should have done that after the first bunch of flowers. She would have felt silly if it had turned out to be nothing, but that was better than feeling like this.

Completely and utterly freaked.

What about Jed? You should tell him.

No. Jed would lose it and he needed to concentrate. She was all right. Those kids might not be.

More knocking on the door. Who the hell could that be? She walked out of the bathroom and grabbed the bat she'd taken to keeping close by her. Especially when she was sleeping. Well, trying to sleep. Maybe it was time to learn how to shoot a gun. Maybe she should go visit Sylvie for a few days until Jed got back. Not that she'd heard from her sister in over a week. And three more emails to Bradley had gone unanswered. She took a calming breath. She had other things to worry about.

She could also have called Ellie. Yeah, there were a lot of things she could have done in the past couple of days.

Dumb. Really dumb.

The bad thoughts that Jed had managed to pretty much chase

away were back with a vengeance and her thigh was bruised from her pinches.

She was a basket case.

She glanced out the side window and when she saw who was standing there, she started to sway with relief. Oh, he looked worn out. He was frowning down at something he held in his hand, but she didn't pay that much attention.

She should have.

She swung the door open, forgetting the bat in her hand. "Jed! You're home!"

He glanced up at her. The look on his face so cold, it made her breath catch in her throat. He was looking at her like he loathed her. "J-Jed?"

"What took you so long to answer the door?"

"W-what?"

"Is there someone in there?" he snapped. There was no warmth in his voice. It was pretty much devoid of any emotion.

"N-no. Why would you say that?" Something was wrong. Very wrong. Her instincts were screaming at her. Why was he looking at her like that? Like she'd betrayed him?

"What's this?" He held something up by his finger, staring at it with disgust. She stared at it as well. It was a flimsy piece of lingerie. Red, see-through and obviously cheap. Why would he have that?

"I-I. . . that's not mine."

"It was sitting on your doorstep. With a note." He held up a piece of paper then read from it. "I saw this and thought of you. Wear it for me tonight, sexy."

No. No, no, no.

"I don't want it," was all she managed to say.

He raised an eyebrow. "Whoever he is, he doesn't have good taste. Or know your size since this is two sizes too big. He should have put it in a bag or a box if he didn't want me to see it. If you're gonna cheat on me, I'd have thought you'd be more discreet than this."

She swayed, unable to hear anything more due to the ringing in her ears. She went hot then cold.

"You think I'm cheating on you," she whispered in horror.

"Think that's pretty obvious, babe." This was the first time he'd called her babe and it hadn't sent a shiver of desire through her. Instead, this babe was almost spat at her. She placed her hand over her nauseous stomach. "You don't get lingerie from strangers who then tell you to wear it for them."

"Y-you don't know what's going on. Y-you're wrong—" She was so upset by the way he was reacting that she couldn't get out what she needed to say. Not that it seemed he wanted to listen.

"Yeah, well, I was wrong about you before, wasn't I?" he said bitterly.

Right. Because he thinks you cheated on him. And now, he's willing to believe the worst of you.

Why hadn't she forced him to listen?

She licked her numb lips. "Jed, listen, y-you don't understand."

"I understand. Don't worry, I blame myself. I shouldn't have gotten involved with you again. I thought you had changed. I was wrong. It happens. Guess at least it happened this time before you got your claws in too deep."

Claws? He thought she had claws? And she'd thought they were already deep. At least she was. Seemed he hadn't felt the same.

"Bye, Daisy. Maybe this time you'll take my advice and leave. There's nothing here for you."

This couldn't be happening. She grasped hold of the door to hold herself up, her grip on the bat loosening. It dropped to the floor but she ignored it, her full attention on the man she loved more than anything.

He turned away.

"Wait, Jed, please. You're wrong. You don't understand."

Why hadn't she told him about the flowers? Or the guys at JSI? *Idiot.*

"Please," she called out, her voice breaking.

But he ignored her. He climbed into his truck. Then he drove away. Leaving her standing there on her porch.

Alone.

As soon as she realized that, she stepped back inside and quickly shut and locked the door. Her heart racing, she ran around the house pulling all the blinds.

That asshole was out there somewhere. She didn't know if he was watching right now, but she wasn't taking any chances. She was alone. All she had was herself.

And she was pretty damn certain that wasn't enough.

When everything was locked up tight, the drapes all pulled, she grabbed the bat and crept over to her secret stash of candy. Yes, she wasn't supposed to have any candy that Jed didn't know about. But a girl needed stuff for emergencies. And besides, wasn't like he was here anymore. These past few days, her appetite had been nil, so she'd been living on suckers. She grabbed a raspberry sucker and popped it into her mouth. Then she picked up the bat again and retreated to that same corner she'd hidden herself in last week behind the sideboard.

She slid down onto her ass, her back leaning against the wall and sobbed.

FUCK. Fuck.

He bashed his fist against the steering wheel as he drove. What had he been thinking to get involved with her? He should have known this would happen again. Should have expected it.

He'd fucking trusted her again and she'd let him down.

You're wrong.

Her voice swam through his head and he growled. He didn't fucking need this. He needed to get home and sleep. He was exhausted. He shouldn't be driving. But something pulled at him. What was he missing?

With a frown, he pulled off to the side of the road. What was it? With how exhausted he was, it was hard for him to think properly. But his gut was telling him something was off.

The baseball bat.

His heart leapt into his throat. Why would she need a baseball bat to answer the door? Her pale features. Could have been because she'd been caught, but she looked like shit. Like she hadn't been sleeping. Worn and scared.

She was scared.

No, terrified.

Fuck. Fuck.

He did a U-turn and pressed down on the accelerator. He needed to get back to Daisy fast because something was very, very wrong.

13

W here the hell was she? He'd knocked on her door. Repeatedly. And he was running out of patience. For some reason, all the curtains and blinds were pulled across the windows. Upstairs as well as downstairs. And she rarely drew the curtains upstairs.

Finally, his worry got too much and he raced around to the back door. Ellie would understand him breaking a window and it was better to do it back here. He picked up a hefty rock and smashed it through the window by the back door. Then pulling off his jacket, he wrapped it around his arm so he could knock out the bits of glass.

Inside, he heard a scared cry as he carefully climbed through the window. He quickly raced in. "Daisy? Daisy!"

His instincts screamed at him, just as he saw a flash of movement. He dropped and rolled, the baseball bat just missing his head. Fuck! That was close.

"Stay away from me, you creep!" Daisy screamed, racing at him, the bat raised.

She was in too much of a panic to see that it was him. At least he hoped that was the reason she was still coming after him and not because she wanted to bash his brains in.

"Daisy, it's me! It's Jed." He didn't want to panic her further by taking the bat off her, even though he easily could. He ducked back as she swung.

"Daisy-girl! Put the bat down!"

Another swing. Shit!

"Daisy! Sugar. It's me, Daddy. It's Daddy. You're safe now."

It was still so new to her that he didn't know if that would work. But suddenly she stopped and stared at him, the baseball bat dropping. Seemed that did work.

"D-daddy?"

She sounded so terrified it made him feel ill. And furious. At whoever had caused this. And at himself, for making it worse. For not listening to her. For jumping to conclusions.

You had reason to believe she was capable of cheating on you.

He watched as she deflated and she slid to the floor. As though she didn't have the strength to hold herself up anymore.

She pulled her legs up and secured her arms around them, making herself into a tight ball.

Fuck. Fuck.

"Jed? Why are you here? I thought you had gone." Her voice sounded lifeless. Dull. Now that he could push past his anger and actually see what was right in front of him, he could tell she was in trouble. Her hair was dull and lank. Her skin a sickly-gray color. Deep chestnut-colored marks lay beneath her eyes. She had on a baggy t-shirt and pants, but he was betting she'd lost weight.

What the hell was going on?

"I did. And that was a big mistake. Realized it almost as soon as I left. Turned around and came back." He crouched down, not reaching for her. Not yet.

"You broke the window."

"You weren't answering the door. I was worried about you."

"Why?" she asked. "I'm just some slut who's cheating on you. A white-trash whore who'd end up embarrassing you."

Where the hell had she gotten that from? He stared at her in shock. Then he was done with this distance between them. Reaching out, he grabbed her, sat back on his ass and pulled her onto his lap. It worried him that she didn't even fight him. As though she didn't have the energy. Or simply didn't care.

"What's going on, Daisy?"

"Now you want to know?"

He hated the bitter tone to her voice. This part was entirely his fault. He grasped hold of her chin and tipped her face up. "I know you're upset with me, baby. And I totally get why. I messed up. I made a mistake. And as tough as it is sometimes to own your mistakes, I'm trying to do that now. I jumped to conclusions and I'm so sorry, baby girl. I will do whatever it is I have to in order to make up for my behavior just before."

There was silence. Shit. He wasn't getting through to her.

Then she shifted on his lap and her eyes met his. He hated the pain he saw in there.

"Anything?"

"Anything," he swore.

"You'll stop spanking me?"

"Yes," he said without hesitation.

She blinked. It was clear she hadn't expected that answer. "Didn't think you'd agree to that."

The hard knot of worry eased inside him. She still had a guarded look on her face, but at least she wasn't completely closed off from him, or trying to hit him with a baseball bat.

"If it's what you need from me and it's in my power to give it to you then I'm going to do whatever I have to in order to give you that." Not that he truly thought she needed him to stop spanking her. It was a test. One he prayed he was passing. But he had something else to impart as well. Something he hoped would tip the scales in his favor.

"I love you, Daisy-girl."

She sniffled. "No, you don't."

"Yes, I do."

"You think I could cheat on you!" she wailed.

Pain blossomed in his chest.

"Obviously, I still have some issues. I jumped to conclusions I shouldn't have. I had to take a moment to think and I quickly realized that I was completely out of line. In my defense, I haven't slept more than a handful of hours since I left you. Wanting to get back to you quickly, I didn't stop to sleep or eat. When I got here, I found cheap lingerie and some sort of love note to my woman on her porch and it flipped something inside of me. But I hurt you and those excuses don't mean shit in the face of that. I'm here to protect you, not be the cause of your pain."

"It's only been two weeks; you can't love me."

"It's been ten years."

She sniffled. "You've loved me for ten years?"

"Yes, I never stopped, baby. Not ever. I love you more now than I did yesterday. I'll love you more tomorrow than I do today. And when our lives end, I'll have loved you enough for a thousand lifetimes and still, it won't be enough."

Tears dripped down her cheeks and her body seemed to just deflate. He had to tighten his hold to hold her up.

She clung to him, as she leaned her face against his chest. "I love you too. And I don't want you to stop spanking me. I kind of, well, it makes me feel good knowing that you care enough to have rules and enforce them. I never had that."

"I know, baby."

"I'm not cheating on you. I never have."

He stiffened against her. "Sugar, we don't need to talk about this—"

She pulled back against his hold and glared up at him, her look so fierce it made him pause. "Yes, we do. Because not talking about it is part of the reason this happened. I have wanted to explain. To apologize. For never being brave enough to go against your grandfather and tell you what really happened."

His grandfather?

That sick feeling in his stomach grew. "What does my grandfather have to do with anything?"

"He's the reason I left."

14

Daisy took in a sharp breath as he rose to his feet then pulled her up with him, not letting go of her hand as he walked into the living room. Then he strode over to the curtains.

"No, don't pull them!" she screeched. He paused and looked down at her. "He's watching me."

"Who is?" He scowled. The air in the room filled with his fury. He placed his hands on her shoulders. "Who is out there?"

"My stalker."

"Your stalker?"

She couldn't read his facial expression clearly. "Yes. He's been sending me flowers. Started two days after you left. I thought it was a neighbor. Until the next two bunches arrived. Then last night there was a note. He must have come back and left that lingerie." She licked her lips. "He's been watching me undress and he wants me to wear it for him."

He said nothing. Just stared at her. Did he not believe her? What was he thinking? Then he turned and strode towards the door. Was he leaving? Tears dripped down her face as she watched him. Then she gasped as he pulled back his fist and smashed it into the wall. Plywood split, small pieces went flying as he drew his hand back. He then leaned both hands on the wall and dropped his head.

"Jed?"

More silence then he turned and the fury on his face made her breath catch in her throat. He paced back and forth.

"Fuck. Fuck! You're being fucking stalked by some sicko and I didn't even know? I accused you of cheating on me? I fucking left you here on your own, so terrified you tried to smash my head in with a baseball bat. A damn baseball bat to protect you! It's my job to protect you. Mine."

And he thought he hadn't done his job. Which would kill a man like Jed. Someone who prided himself on looking after those he considered his.

What the hell did she say to that?

"It's my fault. I didn't tell you."

"I wasn't here for you."

"Jed, you have an important job to do."

He turned his head to look at her, his eyes intense. "Nothing is more important than you."

She gulped. She'd never had that. Not once.

"Those kids needed you."

"So did you."

"But I'm an adult."

"You're a woman living alone being terrorized. Fuck! Fuck!"

She'd never seen him like this and it kind of scared her. Not because she thought he would hurt her, but she was worried about what he was doing to himself.

"There's going to be times you have to work. You can't be here all the time."

"You didn't call JSI."

She shook her head. "I was going to, after the note arrived last night."

"Should have called them after you got that first bunch of flowers. Should have called me. That was one of your rules, Daisy. To call me if you were in trouble."

"I know," she whispered. "But you had to concentrate on what you were doing. And I didn't think anything of the first bunch of flowers. I thought they were from a neighbor. Then the second bunch arrived and I didn't know what to think. It wasn't until the first note arrived that I realized that this could be dangerous. I was going to call JSI. I promise. And no matter what you say, those children were more important. I was fine."

"Not to be mean or anything, babe, but you do not appear fine. You're carrying around a baseball bat in your own house. A house where you have all the curtains pulled. You look like you haven't slept in days or eaten, I'm guessing. And you have fear in your eyes. Something I never wanted to see."

"Not something I ever wanted to feel either."

He took in a shuddering breath. She needed something to diffuse the situation. She looked at the hole in the wall. "Should I be worried about your tendency to make holes in things?"

"What?" He frowned at her.

"Not that I'm sad to say goodbye to the window." She shook her head. "It was a bitch to clean."

"Baby, I'm not going to break anything else."

"You sure? Because the toilet has been a real pain in the ass lately." Her lips actually twitched. There was nothing to really laugh about. Her life was a mess. She had a stalker. She was terrified. Her man had just put his hand through a wall and was now dripping blood on the wooden floors.

But he was here. He was here and she wasn't alone.

"I'm not alone," she whispered.

"Come here, Daisy-girl. Please, baby." She walked over to him and he pulled her close. "I'm sorry for earlier. And you were right, the past is something we need to talk about. Especially the part about my grandfather. But right now, that's not the most pressing thing we need to deal with. We need to figure out what the hell to do about this mess."

"I'm sorry. You've just come home. You're exhausted. You probably just want to eat and sleep and now you've got all this to deal with."

He drew her back, his hands on her shoulders as he gave her a firm look. "Baby girl, listen to me well. None of this is your fault. Understand? None of it. You didn't ask for this asshole to start creeping on you, this is all on him. Not you. Got it?"

She took a deep breath, let that settle in. It wasn't her fault. She hadn't done this. She didn't know who was doing this or why. She couldn't figure it out.

But Jed was here now. He would help her. She wasn't alone.

"All right. Only, what are we going to do?"

He frowned. "Have you still got the stuff he left?"

"Yeah, in here." She took hold of the hand that wasn't bleeding and led him into the kitchen. They passed the baseball bat and she reached down and picked it up. "We need to secure that window."

"I'll take care of it." He lifted the bat from her hand and carried it into the kitchen, setting it down on the table, next to the flowers. She hadn't kept them in vases after the first bunch so they were a little worse for wear. "I didn't want to throw them out as they were evidence. I looked up how to deal with a stalker and it said to gather all the evidence possible."

"I'm guessing it also said to call the police, yes?" he asked gently.

"Yeah. I suppose I didn't want to think I had a problem worth calling the cops about." A wave of dizziness washed over her.

He pulled out a chair. "Sit down. I don't like your color. When is the last time you ate?" He poured her a glass of water.

"Can't eat. It just keeps coming back up when I do."

"Need to get you checked over by a doctor."

"I'm okay. I just haven't slept that great and that note I found last night rattled me. I don't know when he left the second one. Maybe this morning."

She pointed out the piece of paper which she'd turned over so she didn't have to see the words. He flipped it over. Then he went still. His anger filled the room once more. Filling it. Sucking out all the oxygen.

"If you need to hit something, maybe you should use the same wall."

"What?" He stared at her.

"Contain the damage to one area."

He grabbed the back of his neck. "I'm sorry I did that, baby. I shouldn't have. And I'm not going to punch anything else. Well, not until we find this guy. That fucking shithead. I'm going to kill him."

"I should try and stop you but I've had the same thought," she whispered.

"You didn't do too badly with that baseball bat, babe. But we need to work on your technique. How come you even have that?"

"I've owned it for years. We never lived in good areas. Usually the doors were shit protection. I've always kept it under my bed just in case I needed it."

He swore again under his breath. "I hate that. Hate that you weren't protected. Then and now."

"None of this is your fault. This is on him," she repeated his words back to him. They were both quiet for a moment. "What are we going to do?"

He stared down at the notes for a moment and she watched his hands clench into fists then unclench. "Let's think about what we know about him. He's watching the place. The flowers started after I left. Might mean he knows about me. Knows I wasn't around. So he's watching from close by." He turned thoughtful. "But probably at night when he's got less chance of being detected. Means he may not know I'm back."

"Right. But how does that help us?"

"I need to go hunting."

"H-hunting?" she stuttered out.

He crouched in front of her. "I will find him. Gonna be easier if he doesn't know I'm back or that you're freaked by his note. I need to shift my truck and I need you to pull back the curtains."

"You want him to watch me?"

He cupped her face with one hand. "Baby, I will not let him hurt you. I'm going to call in back-up. They will be with you the entire time. I promise. But honey, we got to go fast if we don't want him to find out what's going on and we want to be in place before nightfall."

"Okay," she whispered.

"Good girl. Going to run out and move my truck. I'll make a call while I'm doing it. I'm going to make it look like I'm storming out. Just in case he's around. Then I'll sneak back in. You think you can be in here alone for a few minutes? Promise, less than ten I'll be back."

She thought about that. Just ten minutes and he'd be back. He was covering his bases in case this person was out there watching right now. A lot could happen in ten minutes, though. Could she handle it? Handle drawing back the curtains so if he was out there he could see in? See her?

"Look at me." He cupped her face. "I pretend to storm out. I get in my truck. I take off. I park it around the block and I come straight back."

"He'll see you come back."

"He won't see me. Before I leave, you go lock yourself in the bathroom with your phone and bat. You don't come out until I knock on the door and you hear me talk, all right?"

"The curtains?" she whispered.

"We do that when I get back. Can you do that, baby?"

"I can do that."

"My brave girl. I won't let anything happen to you."

"I know you won't."

"I'm going to catch him. After this, I won't leave you unprotected at any time. I swear."

15

"You okay there, love?"

She jumped at the words, spoken in a sexy accent. All right? No, she wasn't all right. She was so far from all right she didn't even know how to describe how she was feeling. The man standing in the shadowed corner of the living room, turned from looking out the front window to stare at her where she sat on the sofa.

She had the TV on, but it was muted. It was early evening. She should probably turn a light on. But she didn't want to move.

"Just concentrate on breathing. In then out. Everything is going to be fine. I won't let anyone hurt you."

"I don't even know you," she whispered. He was a stranger. With a surprisingly sexy accent. But she wasn't going to tell him that.

"Macca is a weird name." She needed to focus on something other than the fact that Jed was outside somewhere, hunting her stalker.

Back-up had arrived thirty minutes ago, in the form of three seriously attractive, muscular men. Macca and Bain were inside with her. Kent was outside with Jed.

Thankfully, Bain, who was one of the scariest men she'd ever seen in her life, was upstairs while Macca was acting as her bodyguard, or at least she figured that was what it meant when Jed had told Macca that if she got so much as one scratch, he'd make sure he never fathered any children. Macca hadn't seemed too worried. She was starting to think that nothing much bothered him.

"Macca is because my last name is McKenzie."

"Right." Damn, he had to think she was stupid. Something rattled outside and she jumped.

"Don't panic, baby, nothing is going to happen to you."

"What if he finds out you're all here? What if he sees one of the guys outside?" she asked.

"You know much about what your man does?"

"A bit. I know JSI stands for Jensen Security International and that you guys often help find people or guard them."

"Yep. We have a few Government contracts, do some work overseas. Bodyguard work, some retrieval, tracking down people."

She nodded.

"Your man is the best at what he does," Macca told her. "He's focused. Knows what he needs to do and gets it done. Fucking amazing tracker. Best I've ever seen. But no matter what he does, he excels at it. You think some two-bit stalker in a little town like this has a chance against him? Especially when he's got the three of us at his back? Baby, I feel sorry for this asswipe. Or would have, if he hadn't frightened you so much, you're sitting there white as a sheet and trembling. Honey, he hasn't got a chance. You got me here, Bain upstairs and Jed and Kent out there. It's the dream team, baby."

Ridiculously, her lips twitched. "Dream team, huh?"

He pounded at his chest with his fist. "Hell yeah."

She just shook her head, but she had to admit to feeling better.

"Roger that," Macca said. She turned to look at him. She knew he wasn't talking to her. All of the men had ear pieces and were armed.

Macca looked over at her. "Bain's coming down. Daisy?"

She was so tense that even her teeth ached. "Yes?"

"Jed thinks he's found the place where this bastard has been holing up. There's signs of someone camping out in one of the large trees in your yard. Found some gum wrappers. Some footprints."

"But he wasn't there."

"No, but we know where to look. Jed says you usually go to bed at ten?"

"Yeah."

"Probably this guy knows that. You should stick as close to routine as possible. We'll keep the curtains open but don't stand directly in front of the windows. What would you usually be doing about now?"

"Umm, I'd usually work until around nine then watch some TV."

His eyebrow rose. "Working? At this time of night? Screen time right before bed ain't something I'd ever allow. Surprised Jed does."

She scowled at him. "I changed my mind, your accent isn't sexy, it's annoying."

He huffed out a laugh. She looked over her shoulder as Bain entered the room, standing in the doorway. Not that she'd heard him move, she'd just felt him.

Knowing she wouldn't be able to work, she pretended to watch TV for a while, until it grew truly dark. She turned on a floor lamp and, combined with the fairy lights on the mantel they provided enough light for her to see. Macca kept to the shadows. Bain had come downstairs; he was keeping watch out the dining room window.

"This waiting stuff sucks."

She was worn out. But at the same time, she was wired and knew she wouldn't sleep.

"Lie down on the couch, baby," Macca told her. "You can go up to bed soon."

"I won't sleep."

"You can rest."

"What if he doesn't show? Are we going to have to do this again tomorrow night?" How the hell would she get through this night after night?

"Tomorrow, we install cameras around the house. When Jed can't be here one of us is. We'll catch him, Daisy."

Nope. No way. She didn't want strangers in her house.

"I don't want to be a bother."

"First time you received those flowers, you should have told Jed," Bain told her. "You couldn't get hold of him; you should have told us. We could have had cameras on this place, gotten him well before now."

"Bain." Macca frowned over at him.

"Now, you got to put up with someone with you at all times to make you safe then that's what you have to deal with. Jed's not here, one of us is. You need to go somewhere, then someone is on your ass protecting you. Deal."

Wow. Someone who was even blunter and growlier than Jed. She didn't think it was possible.

Macca grimaced. "We normally don't let him speak to clients. He tends to scare them off."

"I'm not a client." She very much doubted she could afford their rates.

"No. You're family," Bain told her. Then he grunted and stiffened. "Jed's caught sight of someone approaching. They're gonna see if he heads to the spot."

"Right, baby," Macca told her. "It's show time. Let's head

upstairs and lure this guy in. Last thing we want is to scare him off by doing anything differently. But you do what I tell you, yeah?"

"What if he's got a gun? What if he hurts someone?" she asked, her voice trembling.

"What'd I tell you about your man, Daisy?"

"That he's a badass."

Bain snorted.

"Didn't quite put it like that," Macca said with a grin. "But yeah, baby, he's a badass."

"He's gonna have your balls, he hears you calling his woman baby," Bain warned.

"That's okay. I like to live dangerously. Let's go."

She walked up the stairs.

"Wait until I'm in the bedroom and in position until you turn on the light."

She nodded at him. Macca slipped inside the bedroom, moving silently. "Walk in here, baby. Then make your way to the bathroom like usual."

She switched on the light as he'd told her. Then she walked over to the attached bathroom and switched that light on.

"He's up the tree," Macca told her in a low voice. She stiffened, as she stood in the bathroom, waiting. It seemed like forever, but it was probably less than a minute before she heard Macca say, "Jed's got him!"

Her heart leaped in her throat and she had to grasp hold of the sink. Her legs shook. Macca stepped into the doorway with a big grin. It faded when he saw her.

"Jesus, Daisy. It's all right now. It's over."

"Is Jed all right?"

"Of course he is. Takedown was easy. Guy wasn't even aware Jed was there. Too busy getting his binoculars out of his backpack to spy on you, the fucker. He wasn't armed. Didn't even put up a fight."

"I need to see Jed."

He studied her, nodded. "He'll be up soon as he can. Why don't you come downstairs? I'll make you something to drink."

"I don't need a drink."

"You sure look like you do. Come with me, Daisy." His voice suddenly deepened. Funny Macca was gone and in his place was a commander. Who wasn't someone you should disobey. She stepped forward and took his hand. She let him lead her out of the bedroom and downstairs. Suddenly, she was in her living room, looking around it as though she'd never seen it before.

Jed had caught him. She'd been living this nightmare for days. Felt unsafe in the one place she should feel safest. And in a few hours Jed had made everything all right. She felt dazed.

"Bain, Daisy needs a drink."

"Chocolate," she whispered. "There's chocolate milk in the fridge."

Macca's eyes warmed for some reason. "Okay, baby. Chocolate milk it is. Come sit." He led her to the sofa and helped her sit. Then he sat on the coffee table in front of her.

"Jed's really all right?"

"He's fine," Bain answered then handed her a glass filled with chocolate milk. "Just getting a few answers from this guy."

"Thanks," she managed to get out without looking at Bain. Then she tipped the glass up and drank it in five big swallows.

She took a breath. "I need another."

Macca's eyes widened. "You really like your chocolate milk, huh?"

She felt herself blushing. They must think she was an idiot. When Macca had said she needed a drink, he'd probably meant an alcoholic one.

What kind of grown woman drank chocolate milk?

"Um..."

"No need to be embarrassed." Surprisingly, it was Bain who

spoke. His voice was rough but he was gentle as he grabbed the glass from her hand. "I'll get you some more."

"Should we call the police? Does Jed know the person?" she asked.

"Just waiting to hear, baby," Macca told her. "You know as much as we do."

This time she sipped the glass of milk Bain gave her more slowly. The chocolately goodness wasn't soothing her the way it normally would.

Macca went still, she knew that meant he was listening to whoever was talking to him through the earpiece. He turned to her. "You know a Mike Lyle?"

"Yes, why?" She froze as understanding hit her. "It was him? Seriously?"

"Yep. That's what Jed says. He's going to call the sheriff, get him out here now that he's got a few answers."

She sat there. Stunned. "I can't believe it was him. I went on a date with him."

"A date?" Macca asked as she sat there, her hand on her rolling stomach. She wished she hadn't drunk all that milk now.

"Yes. I met him on an online dating site. We went on one date. Jed interrupted it. I didn't think he was even interested in me. And he didn't seem the type to send me those notes, to hide up a tree and watch me. . .oh God, I'm gonna be ill." She placed her hand over her mouth, her stomach heaving

Suddenly, she was in the air. She only had a few seconds to realize it was Bain holding her before he had her in the downstairs bathroom. He supported her as she lost all of the chocolate milk she'd just drunk. That really hadn't been a good idea. When the spasms stopped and she was shaking like a leaf, he picked her back up, and carried her upstairs.

"W-where are we going?" she asked.

"Figure your toothbrush and stuff are in the upstairs bathroom," he replied gruffly. He held her easily, not showing any strain at carrying her up the stairs. But then his biceps were bigger than her thighs.

He set her down in her much larger bathroom. Then he stood there, staring at her awkwardly. He didn't strike her as the awkward type. He seemed like the kind of guy who was ultra-confident in everything he did. "You need help?"

"No. Thanks. I'm good now." Not really. But she wasn't bad enough to need the hulking man's help.

"Yeah. Okay. Call out if you're not."

"Thanks, I mean that." She reacted without thinking and reached out to squeeze his forearm.

He just nodded and left, shutting the door behind him. Daisy took a moment to try and calm herself. Unfortunately, her mind kept thinking about the fact that she'd gone on a date with that asshole. Who knew what might have happened had Jed not shown up that night? Or what might have happened if he hadn't come back today. She quickly splashed her face with cold water then brushed her teeth.

By the time she was finished, her teeth were chattering and she was freezing. Then the door opened and Jed was there.

"Sugar."

She didn't think. She just threw herself at him. Thankfully, he caught her.

16

"It's over now, sugar. We got him."

He could feel her shaking in his arms. He was shaking himself. How could he have let a fucking stalker get close to her? Terrorize her? She'd been so terrified she'd been carrying around a damned baseball bat for days.

Then to top things off, he'd jumped to the wrong fucking conclusion and thought she was cheating on him.

Yeah, he had some stuff to sort out.

"He confessed to everything. Leaving the flowers and the notes. Following you. Calling you and hanging up."

"That was him too?" she whispered.

He ran his hand through her hair. "Yeah, baby. It was all him."

"Jed?" He glanced up, pulled out of his thoughts to see Macca in the bedroom.

"Yeah?"

"Sheriff is here. Wants to talk to you both."

"Yeah. Right. Give us a minute, will you?"

"Yeah." Macca's eyes were soft as he stared at Daisy. Jed tightened his arms around her slightly.

Mine.

"You're lucky, mate. Hope you know how lucky."

He loosened his hold. He knew. And he wouldn't be letting her go again. No doubt they'd have their ups and downs, but he wasn't walking away from this and he wouldn't let her either. Maybe he'd originally figured he could just work her out of his system, but she'd managed to get deeper under his skin.

And she was there to stay.

He led her out to the bedroom and sat on the bed, pulling her onto his lap. She clung to him.

"I can't believe it was Mike. I can't believe I went on a date with him. What would have happened if you hadn't interrupted our date?"

"It does no good to think of *what if's*, sugar. All that matters is we caught the bastard. He went down easy. Confessed to it all as soon as I got my hands on him. Apparently, he decided after that date that you were his. He saw me around the house, hung back. Then when a few days went by where I wasn't there, he decided that I had left and he started with the flowers. Then the notes. He'd come here in the evenings, camp out in that tree and watch you."

She buried her face into his chest. Shit. Maybe he should have tried to break that to her more gently. But he was so fucked off that he hadn't protected her better that he wasn't capable of filtering his mouth. What if he hadn't returned home for a few more days? What if he hadn't realized something was wrong and turned around? Would this guy have stepped things up?

Undoubtedly. And despite the fact that he was out-of-shape and unarmed, he was a helluva lot bigger than Daisy.

Fuck. Fuck

She needs you to hold your shit together.

"How did I not know he was out there?" she asked, bewildered.

"He only came when it was growing dark. The tree was good cover. No reason you would know, baby."

"I should have told you. Told someone."

She should have. He'd need to talk to her about that again. But not right now. From now on, he was going to make certain she was far better protected.

"Wh-where is he now?"

"Sheriff has him. I know this is a lot to ask of you, but do you think you can talk to the sheriff?"

"The sheriff?" She looked up at him in confusion. He knew she was in shock. He just needed her to keep it together a bit longer.

"He's downstairs. He needs a statement. I can tell him to come back tomorrow if you can't do it."

She seemed to think that over then she shook her head. "No. I want to get it over with. I can do it."

"That's my brave girl." He kissed her lightly. "Come on, let's do this. Then I can focus on taking care of you."

THIRTY MINUTES LATER, Jed said goodbye to the sheriff. He wrapped his arms tightly around Daisy who was sitting in his lap. He didn't bother to get up. Bain was seeing the sheriff out. Turned out Lyle was already known to the sheriff. He had two restraining orders against him already for each of his ex-wives.

Fuck. He really had fallen down on the job of protecting her.

"You need us for anything else?" Macca asked him from where he stood in the kitchen entrance.

"Nah, we're good," he told Macca then glanced down at Daisy. "Or we will be."

Macca nodded. "She did really well. Listened to all my instructions. Could tell she was scared, but she didn't let it get the best of her. Didn't panic. Guessing now she could use a bit of care, though."

"I know." He didn't need Macca telling him how to take care of his girl.

"Hope you do," Macca said cheerfully, but there was a slight warning in his voice. "Daisy, baby?"

He did not like hearing him call her baby. Daisy didn't move. Worry filled Jed and Macca frowned at him. Yeah, he was aware she wasn't really with them and that wasn't good.

Jed took gentle hold of her shoulders to pull her back. She made a funny little noise and tried to bury in closer.

"Sugar, look at me."

Another noise.

"Babe."

Still nothing.

"Daisy, look at me." He forced some steel in his voice. And she stiffened. He leaned in and whispered against her ear. "I just want to see your face, gorgeous. Everything is all right. You're okay."

She took in a breath, leaned back. She was pale. He took hold of her wrist, taking her pulse. It was fast. Macca slipped up close behind her.

"Sure, you'll be right?"

"Yeah, I got her."

Macca reached out and touched her shoulder lightly. She jumped and turned towards him.

"I'll see you later, all right, love? You did real good tonight."

"Th-thanks." She took a breath, straightened her shoulders. Brave, his girl. "And thanks for all your help."

Macca smiled. "Anytime, love. I'm here for whatever you need."

Jed gave him a look but the other man just shot him a big smile. Bastard.

Then everyone was gone and the house was empty. And quiet.

Too quiet. He could sense Daisy was starting to go somewhere else again.

"Baby, I need you to stay with me, all right?" He took her face between his hands.

She stared up at him in surprise. "I am with you."

"Right. Physically. Mentally, your mind is going somewhere else. I should never have let you stay here."

She stared into his eyes; her gaze clear. "You had to. You didn't know where he was watching from. Or who it was. He might have seen me leave. It was the best way to catch him. And hopefully, I'll be able to sleep now that he's caught."

She was completely exhausted, but also wound up. He needed to get her settled down so she could sleep. And there was one way he could think to do that.

"I feel sick. My heart is pounding. I'm still shaking. How can I sleep like this?"

"I'm going to help you." He cupped her face in his hands. "Do you trust me?"

"Yes."

After the way he'd acted, he was certain he didn't deserve her trust. But he would take it. Cherish it. And make certain he never gave her a reason to regret giving it again.

"Adult Daisy might not be able to sleep, but Little Daisy can."

She stilled. Bit her lip. "I don't think I'm in the right headspace."

"That's why I'm here to help. I want to check the house over one more time, make sure it's all shut up."

"I'll come with you," she said quickly.

He wrapped an arm around her. He noticed her feet dragging, how much she leaned against him. They reached the bottom of the stairs and instead of leading her up them, he picked her up, cradling her against him with one arm under her ass, her legs wrapped around his waist, her arms tight around his neck.

"I love when you carry me," she confessed.

"That's good, baby girl, because I really love carrying you." He quickly checked the rest of the windows, with her held against him then carried her into the bathroom. He set her down on the counter.

"Stay there. Gonna run you a bath."

She yawned. "That sounds nice."

He turned on the taps then looked around. "Got any bubbles?"

"Um, yep, in the bathroom cupboard at the back." She shifted and he grasped hold of her waist.

"Told you to stay." He tapped the tip of her nose. "I'm taking care of things tonight."

"How is that different from any other night," she teased, giving him hope she was starting to feel better.

"Seems I haven't been taking care of you as well as I should have been."

"This wasn't your fault, Jed," she told him. "Really. If anything, it was mine."

"How do you figure that one, sugar?" He grabbed the bubble bath and poured some into the tub before putting it away.

"I must have done something to lead him—"

He placed his hand over her mouth. "I'm going to stop you right there, babe. Don't care what the fuck you did and I don't for one-minute think that you did a thing to lead him on but even if you did, he had no right to do what he did. Sending you things, especially those notes. Watching you through the window. Scaring you. Said it once, and I'll say it as many times as you need to hear it to believe it. That behavior ain't right and it ain't on you, it's on him. Got me?"

She looked at him for a moment. "It's not on you either. You couldn't know when I didn't tell you."

"That won't happen again, will it?" he asked sternly.

"No. It won't."

He cupped her face with his hand. "I'm sorry I jumped to the wrong conclusion and stormed off." He clenched his jaw. "I keep thinking about what might have happened if I hadn't come back."

"You did," she whispered. "You came back. And you got him. I'm safe."

He leaned his forehead against hers. And she'd stay that way.

He turned the taps off as she yawned. Yep, she was crashing. Fast. He needed to get her all tucked up into bed and relaxed. He'd need to talk to Kent about some time off. He had some downtime coming after the last job. But a few days wouldn't be enough. His girl needed him here, helping her through this shit.

First things first. Bath. Bed. Sleep.

"Come on, baby girl. Let me help you get undressed." He moved slowly, keeping his voice soft and steady so as not to frighten her.

She surprised him by being co-operative. She'd only let him undress her once before. She would usually scamper into the bathroom to get changed when he was putting her to bed. Still, as exhausted as she was it was understandable that she'd let him take total control.

He might not like the circumstances around it, but he did enjoy the trust she was giving him. He had her sweater and t-shirt off then without lingering to stare, he whisked off her bra.

This wasn't about sex tonight. It was about taking care of his baby.

"What a good girl you are for Daddy," he murmured to her as he helped her stand.

He grabbed hold of her sweatpants and drew them over her hips and down. "Put your hands on Daddy's shoulders while I help you out. Don't want my girl falling and hurting herself."

A very real possibility when she was dead on her feet. She rested her hands on his shoulders and stepped out of her pants. He stood. His cock was already hard, pressing against his jeans.

She needs softness. Compassion. Understanding.

Not his forte, but he'd try to give her whatever it was she needed.

Then he froze. And not due to the sight of her small but plump breasts topped with cherry-colored nipples. Not at the sight of her small waist that nipped in then flared out into surprisingly generous hips given her size. Not even because of that shaved pussy.

Nope he froze when he saw the fucking bruises. Bruises, plural on her right thigh. He crouched down to get a better look. There were small, some had faded to a yellow-brown, others were purple-pink and tinged with blue. He remembered she'd had some slight bruising the last time he'd helped her undress. This was something different entirely.

"Where the fuck did you get these from?"

SHE FROZE. Shit. Shit. Shit. Why hadn't she remembered? Stupid. She'd never intended him to see them. She'd been trying hard to stop, but with Jed away, the voice came back. And then her anxiety over the flowers and notes just seemed to stir things up more. Until her thigh was a mess.

She was so screwed up.

She placed her hand over the bruises, as though hiding them would make him forget that he'd ever seen them.

Jed gently pried her hand away. He just stared at her thigh and she braced herself for his disgust. His horror.

You are such a mess.

"Jed, I can explain."

He stared up at her and the look in his eyes was so dark and cold that she couldn't even breathe.

"Who did this to you?"

She shook her head.

"Don't you fucking protect them," he said in a harsh voice. "Don't even think about it. I want a name and I want it now. Who did this to you?"

She licked her lips, her heart racing.

"Who. Did. This?"

"It's not what you think," she managed to whisper.

He just waited. Stared up at her. And the room filled with his fury. Foreboding. An imminent storm.

She braced. "I did it."

17

He rocked, falling back onto his ass as he stared up at in her shock. It didn't even register that he'd lost his balance or that he probably looked like an idiot.

She. . .she. . .

"You did this to yourself?" he whispered.

Her face was blank as she stared down at him. "Yes."

His mind whirled, trying to process that. Why would someone hurt themselves like that? He managed to pull his shit together when he noticed that she was creeping away from him, watching him with a wariness that told him she thought he was on the edge of exploding.

He got to his feet then wished he'd moved more slowly as she flinched.

"Baby, you're scared of me?" He forced himself to calm his voice. It was obvious she was getting ready to bolt and he really didn't want to chase her through the house.

"No."

He raised his eyebrow.

"I-I'm scared of what you're gonna say or think."

"What do you think I'm gonna say or think?"

"That I'm a freak," she whispered.

Shock stabbed him in the gut. She really thought that?

"Baby—"

"I don't do it all the time," she told him quickly. She'd wrapped her arms around herself defensively. "It's just when I hear his voice, telling me that I'm a slut or worthless or—"

"Who?" He couldn't stop himself from grabbing hold of her arms then cursed himself as she let out a scared cry.

Easy, man.

"Baby, who said those things to you?" Who the fuck did he have to kill?

Her eyes were wide, swimming with tears. It killed him to see her like that.

"I-I don't want to tell you."

He frowned, not liking that. "Babe, if I'm gonna help you I need to know what the fuck is going on."

"I dreamed of one day telling you everything. But I'm a lot braver in my dreams. Never intended for you to know about this, though." She waved her hand at her thigh. "Wasn't ever going to tell you that he haunts me, even before he died."

"Babe, who?" His gut clenched with dread.

"Your grandfather."

SHE BRACED HERSELF.

He'd deny it. Of course, he would. He wouldn't believe her. She'd let him down. He thought she had betrayed him. He loved his grandfather.

He stared at her and she couldn't read his expression. "My grandfather."

"I know you might not want to believe me, but he. . .he. . ." she gulped. "I need to tell you all of it. Will you listen now?"

He nodded. She couldn't read the look on his face, but at least he wasn't calling her a liar and storming out.

"Yeah, I'll listen to whatever you have to say."

Thank God.

"I'll just go get my robe." She made to move but he grabbed her hip, holding her still. "No."

"But I. . .I can't do this naked!"

Without a word, he whipped off his t-shirt and pulled it over her body. She slid her arms into the holes. The scent of him surrounded her. The t-shirt warm from his body heat. And her eyes sort of glazed over as she took in his cut body.

The man was gorgeous. Even in her state, she had to take a moment to admire him. There was no other choice.

"Sugar, my eyes are up here."

She glanced up quickly, totally embarrassed she'd been caught staring.

"Like what you see?"

"You know I do." She rolled her eyes. "How do you not just stand and stare at yourself in the mirror all day? That's what I'd do if I had a body like that."

He laughed. Then he sobered. "Jesus, babe. Got back to town today, dying to see you, absolutely exhausted after the hell of the last few days only to find some asshole has been stalking you. I had to watch you hold it together by the skin of your teeth, bring you up here to take care of you the best way I know how only to find you been fucking bruising yourself because my bastard grandfather has done something fucked-up to you. What he's done I don't know and that's screwing with my head, big time."

"It's not. . .he didn't touch me or anything," she whispered.

"Well, that's a relief," he said. "But there are other things I'm imagining, baby, and I need to know if they're true. But in the midst of all that shit and that's a lot of shit to deal with in one freaking day, you manage to make me laugh. And that, as well as a whole lot of other stuff I don't have time to go into is why I love you. Loved you for over ten freaking years, just buried it deep. But it never went away. You've been mine since you were sixteen, our lives just took different paths for a while, but you were always with me. Now it seems my grandfather might have had something to do with that. So please, will you just tell me."

She stared at him for a moment, then nodded. "I'll tell you. All of it."

HE CLOSED the lid of the toilet and sat then pulled her onto his lap.

"Um, you don't think we should go downstairs to talk?"

"Nope." He needed this done and he wasn't giving her time to change her mind or try to soften the story.

"Okay. In all the ways I'd imagined I'd tell you this it wasn't while sitting on the toilet. With a bare butt."

"Usually the way one would sit on a toilet, I'd think," he teased her to ease the tension even though he wasn't finding anything humorous about this situation. But he felt her relax slightly. He ran his hand up and down her back.

"Babe," he prompted when she remained silent for a while.

"I'm scared to tell you," she whispered. "Over the years I thought about this moment. About what I would say. About how you would react."

"Well, I can help you with that last part." He drew her back so he could stare down into those deep, gray eyes. "I can't guarantee I won't lose my shit. That I won't punch another wall. What I can tell you is no matter what you tell me, I will not leave you. Ever. You're in me now. You're my love. My girl. Might have lost my mind earlier and stormed out, took me less than fifteen minutes to realize I'd fucked up big and come back. That was fifteen minutes too many. Ain't going anywhere and neither are you."

She took a deep breath, let it out slowly. "Right."

He could tell she didn't quite believe him still. But he would show her.

"It was about two months after you left. A Saturday night. Sylvie was staying over with a friend. Brad was out. And every Saturday I could, I tried to go to our place."

Their place was a pond on his grandfather's estate. He'd lived with his grandfather after his parents were killed in a helicopter accident. His grandfather hadn't exactly known what to do with a five-year old boy. Jed's grandmother had died of cancer years ago. Jed had mainly been raised by a nanny. It hadn't been a terrible experience. He'd been given whatever he desired. But it hadn't been a warm, loving household. All of the men in Jed's family had served at one time and his grandfather had been happy at his decision to enlist. Jed had mainly enlisted so he had a shot at building something for him and Daisy.

"I was sitting there, thinking of you when I heard someone approach. I turned and there was Bobby. I didn't know him that well. We'd barely even talked. I said hello. He smiled back and said, hello, sexy. Then he walked up and sat beside me. Too close. I tried to move away and he flung an arm over my shoulders. He said he'd been watching me, waiting to catch me alone. Told me I was hot and I deserved better than you."

That fucking asshole. Hitting on his girl. But he bit back his growl of anger. He needed to hear the rest of this.

"I told him to let me go. To leave. That I loved you. He wouldn't leave, though." A sob escaped her and he stiffened.

No, please God, no.

"He wrapped his arms tight around me and kissed me. I tried to fight back but he had me pinned. Then he whispered at me that this might be a job, but he was gonna enjoy fucking me. He was going to rape me. I tried to fight. But he was stronger. He was determined. He had me on the ground, was tearing at my clothes."

She let out a sob and he pressed his lips to the top of her head, his eyes closing. Tears threatened.

Keep it together.

Fuck. Fuck him. Fuck Bobby.

"Sh, baby." Anger burned so bright inside him that it was an inferno. Much as he didn't want to know what happened, she needed to give it and he had to take it. For her. He had to take some of that poison away and shoulder what pain he could.

She went still. Quiet. He knew she was back there and that wouldn't do. He needed the story. But damned if he wanted her reliving it while she told him. He tipped her back, gently grasped hold of her chin. "Baby girl, look at Daddy. Look at Daddy."

"I can't," she whispered brokenly.

"You can. Look at me." She stared up at him. "I'm here. I'm not going anywhere. You're with me. Jed. Daddy."

"Daddy," she repeated.

"That's right, baby girl."

"My bubble bath will get cold."

"I'll draw you a new one then."

"A new one. Okay. We'll make a new one."

"Tell me the rest, sugar," he urged. He needed to hear it and she needed to get it out.

"The rest." She drew in a deep breath. "I thought he was going to rape me. There was nothing I could do. And then I heard this cry. And then a thump. Bobby's eyes rolled back in his head and he dropped on top of me. I was hysterical. I didn't know what was happening. I looked up and saw Brad's face."

"Your brother?" His voice was hoarse.

"Yes. He knew I went to the pond on Saturdays and he'd come looking for me. He wanted money for-for something. He heard me scream. Saw what was happening and he picked up this big branch and hit Bobby over the head. He was pale, shaking and his terror helped me pull myself together. We got Bobby off me and then we just ran." She shook her head. "We didn't even stop to see if he was alive. We just took off."

"Good," he said fiercely. "He didn't deserve any care. But how does this have anything to do with my grandfather?"

And why would she have left town with Bobby if he'd nearly raped her? Although he already knew the answer to that. She wouldn't.

Yeah. Fuck him.

"We raced until we got back to our place. Mom wasn't there. Sylvie wouldn't be home until the next day. Brad wasn't in a good way. . .I made him a hot chocolate. I told him he did the right thing over and over. He crashed in bed and then I. . .I lost it. I showered for a long time. Until the water went cold. And I cried. A lot. I was about to climb into bed even though I didn't think I would sleep and I was wishing for once that Mom was home, there was this knock on the door." She tensed. "It was your grandfather."

He braced. "And?"

"I thought maybe someone found Bobby. Maybe he was dead. Maybe Brad killed him. I was shaking as I opened the door. He was so calm. So cold. He told me that he wanted me gone. Out of town. Out of your life. Bobby. . .Bobby wasn't dead. But your grandfather had found him. He knew he was there. He sent him."

"He sent him?" He couldn't process what she was telling him.

She ran a shaking hand over her face. "He had these photos. I. . .I swear I fought him, Jed. I did. I didn't want him. . ."

"Baby, hush, I know you didn't." His frozen state melted at the fear in her voice.

"But the photos. . .some of them looked like I was participating. I don't know how he even had the photos."

"They set it up," he whispered.

"Yeah," she whispered back. "Took me a long while to figure that out. Not until we were gone from that town. Not until I could think of that night without having a panic attack. I don't know if he took the photos himself—"

"No way. He had lackeys for that shit. Somehow, he got Bobby to attack you, but to pin you in such a way it didn't look like you were fighting. Must have had someone in the bushes, taking photos."

"They. . .they weren't the worst of the photos."

"What?"

"They'd also taken photos of Brad hitting Bobby. Then of us fleeing the scene. Your grandfather, he said it didn't look good for me, but it really didn't look good for Brad. That Bobby had a concussion, was in the hospital and that the sheriff was ready to take a statement. The sheriff who was really good friends with your grandfather."

He'd arranged the whole thing. Jed couldn't believe any of this. It felt like this was a dream. A story she was telling about something that had happened to someone else.

Not his girl.

"He said that both of us would be arrested. Brad for assault. Me for fleeing the scene. And for theft."

"What fucking theft?"

"I asked him that, and he pulled out Bobby's wallet. Said that Bobby could give a statement where I lured him out to the pond and came on to him then my brother hit him and we stole his wallet. That the photos of Brad hitting Bobby would be sent anonymously to the sheriff. But if I did what I was told, Bobby would tell everyone he had no idea who hit him."

"That fucking asshole."

"I said I would tell the truth. That Bobby attacked me. He asked me who I thought everyone would believe? The son from one of the most respected families in the county? Or the criminal daughter of the town whore."

"Criminal? You fucking stole once to feed your brother and sister."

"It doesn't matter," she whispered. "He was right. No one would believe me. Especially not the sheriff. He hated us and was good friends with your grandfather. He asked me what he thought would happen to Sylvie if I wasn't around? How long it would take before Child Protection Services took her away? I couldn't let that happen to Sylvie. You know about the last time we were taken in by CPS."

He tightened his hold on her. Yeah, he fucking knew. And he couldn't believe his grandfather would pull that on her. He had to know she would do whatever was needed to keep Sylvie out of care. When she was fourteen, she'd stolen some food because they hadn't eaten for days. Unfortunately, she'd been caught. The sheriff had called in Child Protection Services, they'd found her mom two towns over, stoned. And they'd taken all three kids into care.

"Sylvie didn't speak for two months after we got her back," she whispered. "Brad, he came back with bruises everywhere. I couldn't let that happen to them again. I had to protect them."

"I know you did, baby." He hated that all of that had been on her slim shoulders. That she'd had to make that choice. Had been forced to make it.

"I asked him what he wanted. He told me it was simple. He wanted me gone. Out of your life. That I was going to leave and I was never to contact you again. That if I did that, he'd make sure that nothing came back on Brad and me."

The anger was so huge his insides were burning.

"I told him you'd try to follow me. Find me. He just smiled. Then he said I was going to leave a note, telling you I'd fallen in love with Bobby and that I never wanted to see you. Then I was to pack up everything, including my family, and go. That if I stayed away forever, then my brother would be protected and those photos would never be leaked. If I tried to contact you, he'd have no choice but to have Bobby change his statement."

"I cannot fucking believe it."

She tried to pull away from him, but he held her tight. "It's true!" There was a hint of hysteria in her voice as she pushed at his chest.

"Baby, I didn't mean I didn't believe you. Hush. Calm down before you hurt yourself. I believe you. Every word. I just cannot believe he would do this. To me. To you."

She slumped. As though all her energy had drained out of her. "He hated me. He said that he'd waited for you to tire of me. That he would never accept some white trash, worthless, daughter of a whore into his family."

He gathered her tight, rocked her. "Baby. Baby."

"I knew he didn't like me. . .but I never realized. . .I don't even know why he suddenly decided I had to go then. . .I've never understood."

"I asked for my grandmother's ring."

"What?"

He stared into the distance. "I called him and asked for her ring and he knew I was going to propose to you when I got back. He pretended to be happy. He must have got desperate. Concocted this fucking scheme to get you out of my life. And I fucking fell for it. He even offered to send a PI after you. To find you. I told him no. Wonder what he would have done if I'd said yes. No doubt he had a plan."

"What happened to Bobby?"

"I don't know," she whispered. "I never saw him again after that night."

"Bobby's old man owed my grandfather something. I never knew what, but my grandfather would talk about the debt sometimes. Bobby was used to pay for it." Didn't excuse what he'd done in any way.

They were silent for a long time while he processed this.

"I thought about contacting you. All the time. About calling you and telling you the truth. But I was scared. I had to protect Brad and Sylvie. I used the money you left me to get us out of there. We were gone less than a week when Mom found some man and left us."

That bitch.

"I was all they had."

"I know, baby."

"When they were older, out of reach of CPS, I looked you up. Couldn't help myself. That's when I saw you were engaged and I knew that I'd do more damage than good with the truth."

They were both silent, thinking.

"Part of me thought he was right."

He stiffened. "What?"

"I wasn't ever good enough for you, Jed. I was a criminal. A thief. I lived in a trailer—"

He turned her so she faced him, her legs straddling his. He had to fight the urge to shake her. "That's bullshit! You were everything to me. You were beautiful, sweet and kind. You still are. And I won't stand for you saying bad things about yourself. You weren't good enough for me? You were everything that was light and sweet and good about my world. You best not talk badly about my girl."

Tears flooded her eyes. "I try to fight his voice. To tell myself that none of what he said about me was true. Mostly, I'm successful. Sometimes I'm not." She gestured at her thigh.

His jaw tightened at that reminder of the pain his grandfather still put her through.

Daisy slumped against him. Enough. It was time to take care of his girl. "Baby girl, you need sleep."

"Don't think I can manage a bath."

"Then let's get you into bed." He picked her up and carried her into the bedroom, setting her down briefly on the side of the bed so he could pull back the covers. Then she shocked him by asking a question he didn't expect.

"You really believe me?"

He helped her into bed, then got in after her, pulling her onto his chest. "Of course, I believe you."

"I'm so sorry."

"Daisy-girl, you have nothing to be sorry about."

"I do. He said you wouldn't believe me. That with all the evidence, if I tried to explain you would side with him. I believed him. I shouldn't have."

No. She shouldn't have. But she was seventeen and she'd learned the hard way that people could be assholes. She'd learned to rely on herself. That she had to be the strong one, who made the decisions, who took care of her family. Too much fucking responsibility was laid on those thin shoulders.

"If anyone should be saying sorry, it's me. I left you there. Knowing your world wasn't a great place. My fucking grandfather arranged to have you assaulted then blackmailed you, he kept us apart for ten years. After you left, he told me he thought you were only with me for his money. He warned me that people might come out of my past once I inherited his fortune. That's why I accused you of searching me out for money. Even in death, it's like he was trying to keep us apart."

She reached around and placed her hand over his mouth. "Not your fault, dragon. You didn't know what happened."

But that didn't mean he still didn't feel guilty.

HE GLANCED down at the woman lying in bed, wearing his t-shirt. Damn, if he didn't like that even more than seeing her in those cutesy nighties. She was sucking on the binky he'd bought for her and she looked so young.

Sweet and innocent.

She'd been through hell. He ground his teeth together then grabbing his phone he walked out into the hallway. The whole place needed cameras. A security system. Why hadn't he seen to that already?

Yet another way he'd fallen short.

He brought up Kent's phone number

"Hey, man, everything okay?" Kent's hushed voice sounded through the phone. Then he heard a woman's voice. Abby. "It's all right, sweet girl, go back to sleep."

He winced. There was rustling noises.

"All right, speak," Kent ordered.

"Sorry to wake her, chief."

"It's fine. What's going on? Daisy all right?"

"No," he told him honestly. Then without another word, he laid it all out for his boss. The man who'd taken him in, given him a job, a purpose, a home even though he hadn't really thought of it that way until now. After leaving the Navy, he'd had no idea what he was going to do. He only knew he needed to get out.

Kent had given him all that.

"What do you need?"

And that was the reason he'd given the man his loyalty. Kent always had his back.

"Bobby-John Jones," he bit out. "Can't go after him myself. Can't leave Daisy."

"She comes first," Kent agreed. "I'll send Zander."

That's who he would send. Zander was a damn good tracker, not as good as he was but then he was the best. Zander could be a terse bastard but he had a soft streak for women. There was just one issue.

"I want him alive and in one piece." With Zander, it was a crap-shoot whether that would happen.

Kent sighed. "Want me to send Bain?"

Bain was probably the guy he was closest to. But he wasn't the tracker Zander was.

"No. Just make sure Zander knows he's mine."

"Got it." There were a few beats of silence. "Jed, you have to know it wasn't your fault, what happened to Daisy."

Wasn't it? Then how come there was a boulder of guilt on his shoulders? "I didn't go after her back then. I was nursing my hurt. I should have. Knew it didn't add up but I didn't go find her."

"He was your grandfather. You loved him."

He had. The bastard hadn't deserved it.

"I didn't treat her well when she turned up here. Thought she was after his money."

"It's been ten years. Had to be a surprise."

"Some of the things we've done. . .if I'd known. . .I would have gone gentler."

"I'm thinking if you did anything to scare her, you would have noticed that. I'm guessing she enjoyed whatever you did. Jed, man, you know whether she's talked to anyone? A therapist? 'Cause I'm thinking all this stuff with Lyle stalking her, it might stir things up."

"I don't know."

"If you need someone, I got a friend who lives in Texas. He knows this therapist there who's in the lifestyle. Her husband is the sheriff and her Dom. Apparently, she's good."

"Give me her name." Because he wanted his girl to have whatever she needed.

"I'll call my friend. See if I can pull some strings," Kent told him. "Jed, whatever you need. We're here for you."

"Thanks, chief."

He walked back into the bedroom, strode to the side of the bed and stared down at her. The binky had fallen out, and she was sucking on her thumb. Normally, he'd switch them over but right now he didn't want to deny her anything.

He took a deep breath, let it out slowly as he remembered her telling him about Bobby attacking her. The look of horror on her face when he'd seen her bruised thigh.

Fuck. Fuck.

Breathe through it.

Images raced through his head, one after the other until he knew there was no way he could sleep right now. Instead, he walked to the wall and sat with his back against it. He'd stay here, watch over her, but he wouldn't sleep.

SHE WOKE SUDDENLY, her heart racing.

Something was wrong. Where was she? She breathed deep for a minute then took a look around. Her heart slowed as she recognized the room. Memories rushed back to her. Moany Mike the stalker. Telling Jed everything. Jed putting her to bed.

But there was no Jed next to her.

She sat up slowly then spotted him over by the door. He was sitting, leaning against the wall, his legs pulled up to his chest, his bent arms resting on his knees, the palms of his hands pressed to his eyes.

He looked sad. Almost defeated.

Her stomach tightened into a knot. She'd done this.

"I should never have told you."

He didn't look up. Didn't say anything for a while and her guilt grew.

"I blamed you," he finally said.

"What?"

"I blamed you. For leaving me. Hated you, even. And it was all him."

She climbed out of bed. "Jed."

"I just need a minute, sugar. Stay in bed."

She glanced at the clock beside her. Five in the morning. How long had he been sitting there for?

He still didn't look at her. And she wasn't staying in bed. But still she felt hesitant as she walked over, knelt on the floor in front of him. Her hand shook as she reached out, hoping like hell he didn't reject her. When she touched his arm, he looked at her. Maybe it was a trick of the light, but she swore tears glinted in his eyes.

Oh God. She'd brought tears to her man's eyes.

"Ten years. Ten years he took from us." One of those tears dripped down his face. Tears burned in her eyes and she forced them back. He'd always been strong for her. This time, it was her turn. Her man was hurting and she needed to do whatever she could to help him.

"I know, honey," she said soothingly. "But we're together now."

"And I nearly ruined that. Thought you were here for the money. Didn't take long for me to realize it wasn't that. Then I couldn't get you out of mind. Hard to sleep, to concentrate. Thought I'd buried it all deep. Built impenetrable shields and you blasted right through them. You're so deep in me, don't know where I end and you begin."

"Jed—"

"And I don't wanna know. 'Cause I don't ever intend to pull us apart."

That hurt disappeared.

"I'm here, my dragon. I'm not going anywhere. For the last ten years, I've felt like I've just been going through the motions. When we fled Lawrence, I needed to find a place for us to go. I had to find a job. Had to take care of Sylvie and Brad. Had to deal with Mom leaving us. I used to have panic attacks. Nightmares. I lived half a life. There was always something. Always a decision to be made, a bill to pay, a crisis to overcome. Brad left to go travelling and even though I was happy for him, it left me with Sylvie to take care of.

And she. . .I know I shouldn't talk badly of my sister but she drains me. I knew I had to get away. To do something for myself. I was lost, Jed. Always lost."

She reached out and gently touched his knee. "I'm not lost anymore."

He stared back at her. "No, you're not." He grasped hold of her hand, held on tight.

"Please, God, at least tell me that the man who came after Bobby treated you gentle. That you told him you'd been attacked and he took the time to care for you."

She avoided his eyes.

"Daisy? Jesus, please," he practically begged.

"There hasn't been anyone else," she whispered.

"What?"

She forced herself to meet his gaze. "I've never been with anyone. Those first few years, there was no way I could even think of it. Not without losing it. And then I had no real desire to when all I'd ever wanted was you." She shrugged helplessly.

"You mean you're. . ."

"A twenty-seven-year-old virgin. Yep. Pretty pathetic, huh?"

A fierce look crossed his face. "I never want to hear you call yourself that again, understand?"

"Call myself worse," she whispered.

He reached forward, cupped her face between his hands. "And that's gonna stop. Whatever words you call yourself, whatever you hear him say to you, none of it is true. And I'm gonna replace every bad thought with a good one. Got it?"

She nodded.

"You ever talk to someone about what happened?"

"Not really. Brad knows it all. Sylvie just parts of it. She was too young. As she got older, well, I didn't want her to know."

"You've never talked to a professional about any of this?"

"No."

"Kent gave me the name of a therapist. She knows the lifestyle. She'll do sessions online. She's good."

She stiffened. Talk to a stranger? "I can't."

He studied her for a long moment. "Whether you do this or don't do this, it's up to you. No matter what I'm still going to be here for you. I'll be supporting you with whatever you need. I just want you to be happy."

"You're not gonna make me go?"

"Babe, ain't no point to it if I make you go. You have to want to do this."

"I want to do this. Or, I mean, I want to fix this. Fix me. But I'm scared to talk to a stranger."

He gave a fierce look. "First of all, you aren't broken. Hear me? Your head got messed with by an asshole who I have the misfortune to be related to. The things he said to you are unforgivable and I hate that his words still have the power to hurt you. But you ain't broken. You just need some help to put that voice to rest. If you don't think this woman can do that for you or you're not ready, then I'm not going to force you."

"I thought you might be mad."

"Baby, never. I just want you to be free of those demons, of this power he has over you. I definitely don't want you hurting yourself anymore because that's the only way you know how to free yourself of him."

She'd stared up at him, this wonderful man who was vowing to do whatever it took to help her and she knew she had to be brave. She had to be as strong as he seemed to think she was. She had to do whatever it took to free herself.

"I'm going to do it."

Light filled his eyes. "You're sure?"

"I'm sure. What about you? Will you talk to her?"

"I will do whatever needs doing to help you."

"But to help you."

He dropped his hands then widened his legs. "Come sit here." He patted the floor between his legs. She turned and backed her way in. He wrapped an arm firmly around her chest, surrounding her with him.

"Not real big on talking to a chick about this."

"A chick!" she protested.

"Yeah, a chick." She heard the smile in his voice. Knew he was teasing her. "But if I need to talk, I got Bain."

"Bain?"

"Yeah, Bain."

"Does he know how to talk? Without growling?"

He let out a surprised laugh. She smiled, relaxed against him. "Not really. But he knows how to listen."

"Okay then."

"Okay then," he repeated. Still with amusement in his voice. They sat there for a long moment.

"I'm mad that he's dead. That he's beyond my anger. Everything he took from you—"

"He took it from you as well, Jed."

"Never forgive myself for not trying to find you," he whispered.

"Honey, you have to. You have to let it go."

"Don't fucking know how to do that."

She turned to him. "Together, we do it together." She leaned her forehead in and touched it against his.

"Together," he whispered.

18

The nightmare screamed through her, dragging her from sleep. The way it had every night for the last three nights. Ever since she'd told Jed the truth. Having it all come out was almost as bad as having to live it again.

Almost. Because this time she had Jed. She wasn't alone.

And yet, she didn't have Jed. This was a different Jed than the one she'd had before. This Jed was quieter, most people would probably argue he'd never been much of a talker, but he had been with her. This Jed was gentler. He watched her. All the time.

This Jed hadn't once scolded her. Hadn't given her so much as a stern look. Admittedly, she'd walked around in a haze of exhausted shock for those first few days. She felt fragile. She didn't like it. Discovering she had a stalker, knowing he'd been watching her, feeling scared in her own home she figured it was enough to unnerve the strongest person. Without all of the stuff from the past coming up as well.

Yeah, she was a different Daisy, but she felt a bit more like herself each day. Today, her Little had even surfaced for a while when she'd found the coloring books he'd bought her the other day. And Daddy had even helped.

A subdued daddy.

He hadn't been back to work, hadn't mentioned going back and the truth was, she wasn't ready to be left here alone.

Don't be such a wimp, Daisy. He'll have to return to work at some stage. You can't rely on him forever.

She knew it. But her sense of safety had been rattled and she wasn't sure how to get it back.

She also knew that she missed her Jed. Wanted him back.

He slid his arm around her waist. Carefully. As though afraid she would shatter. That was how he touched her now. Like she might break. There had been no spankings. He hadn't once put his hand in her back pocket of her jeans to guide her around. And there had been no orgasms.

"Bad dream, baby?" he murmured.

"Yes," she whispered.

The first words of the song hit the room. She started to relax. She'd been shocked after her first nightmares, when the dregs of it were still clinging to her, to hear him singing to her. Always the same song. Always low and soft. Always it washed away the nightmare like nothing else could.

He had a gorgeous voice. Soft yet husky, he hit every note of *Amazing Grace* perfectly. There was nothing more beautiful than her fierce dragon, singing her back to sleep in the most tender voice imaginable.

Tears dripped down her face, but she tried not to let him sense them. She didn't want to explain the reason for them. Wasn't sure she could. Wasn't sure he wanted to know it was because she'd never had something as beautiful in her life as him singing to her.

Gradually, the tears dried. Her body relaxed and sleep overtook her.

. . .

JED SLID AWAY FROM HER, lying on his back. He placed his arm over his eyes as he reminded himself that she was fragile. That she needed care. She'd just woken from a fucking nightmare, for God's sake. The last thing she needed was to know that he was lying there with a freaking hard-on.

Only an asshole would think of his own needs now. But he couldn't stop himself from imagining how good it would be to roll her under him and drive himself deep. On the tail of that thought came another. Of Bobby trying to rape her. His grandfather threatening her.

His hard-on died.

She needed gentle loving care. What she did not need was to know how much he wanted to fuck her. She did not need his brand of Dominance. She needed soft and gentle. Not stern and bossy.

And he would give her whatever she needed.

"TELL me you found that fucking bastard." Jed stepped out onto the porch of Daisy's place to where Kent, Bain and Macca stood.

Kent looked behind him. "Daisy around?"

"She's having a nap. She's not sleeping well." She was having fucking nightmares. About an hour ago, he'd seen her yawning and fighting to stay awake as she'd been playing with her Legos and decided to put her down.

Surprisingly, she hadn't argued. Which had told him just how much she needed the nap. He hadn't made her take one since he'd returned. He needed to change that.

"Fuck," Macca muttered. "She messed up over that asshole stalking her?"

He gave a short nod. "That and the past. Just tell me you've got him so I can take my fury out on someone."

They gave each other a look. And a knot formed in his gut.

Kent stepped forward. "I'm real sorry, man. We found him, but he died five years ago. Car accident."

Fuck. Fuck!

"I know this has got to hurt, mate—" Macca started.

"Hurt! Hurt? It doesn't fucking hurt!" He turned to the other man. "My woman, the woman I have loved for ten years was fucking attacked by that asshole! She still has nightmares. She has to fucking hurt herself to try and cope with the memories. To try and wipe away the shit my grandfather said to her that has clung to her for ten years! And both of those fuckwits are dead and beyond my rage!"

"But your woman is still here and she needs you," Kent said quietly.

"And how am I supposed to help her! She doesn't even feel safe in her own fucking home!"

"Bring her back to yours," Macca said.

"That's not a home! It's a place where I sleep. It's weeks away from being somewhere that's worthy for her. It needs to be perfect."

They all looked at each other again.

"Mate, I don't know Daisy all that well, but she doesn't seem the type of girl to worry about perfect," Macca said to him.

"You're right, you don't know her," he said coldly. "If you did, you'd know she's never had special. She's never really had a home. She's taken care of her siblings pretty much since they were born. She never had a chance to be a kid. She'd settled in here. Nestled. She's a homebody. And that bastard took that feeling of safety from her."

"Then give it back," Bain said quietly.

"What?" He turned to the big man.

"Give her that sense of safety back. That's your job, right? As her man."

It was. He let out a breath. How to do that, though?

"Jed?" Kent asked quietly. "Anything you need?"

"Time," he said quickly.

"You got it," Kent replied.

Something else occurred to him. That might work.

"Actually, there's something else I need your help on." Leaning in, he laid it out for them.

19

She plodded down the stairs, not really noticing where she was going. Blankie was under one arm and she was wearing her favorite Eeyore nightie. Okay, maybe naps weren't her favorite thing in the world. But with how little sleep she was getting at night now, they'd become a necessity.

Earlier when Jed had decreed it was time for a nap, she hadn't argued. She'd let him put her to bed, with the pillows arranged around her body so she was all tucked in. Then he'd given her blankie before kissing her forehead and massaging her back until she fell asleep.

He hadn't noticed that her binky was missing. Or pulled her thumb from her mouth. Or reminded her not to get up without him.

Unease had filled her as she'd drifted off, but she'd pushed it aside. He'd had less than a week to come to terms with everything. He didn't have Molly, her amazing therapist, to work things through with. Although she wished he'd talk to someone about it.

Things would get better.

She yawned as she walked into the living room to find him

sitting on the couch. Jed turned, pausing what he was watching on TV as she entered the room.

"Hey, Daddy."

"Little girl, did you walk down the stairs alone?" he asked in a deep voice.

Her tummy danced with nerves and excitement. Maybe she'd been worried about nothing.

"Sorry, Daddy," she mumbled. She waited for him to tell her off. To maybe even take her over his knee and give her a few smacks.

Instead he just shook his head. "Don't do that again."

Disappointment flooded her. She walked over and sat next to him on the couch and plonked her feet on the coffee table. What did a girl have to do to get a spanking around here? Worry and frustration as well as broken sleep were making her grumpy.

"Disney channel, Daddy," she demanded.

He turned to her, raised an eyebrow. "Excuse me?"

"Wanna watch the Disney channel."

"There's a game on, baby."

She stuck her lower lip out. That sucked. She sighed. Long and loud. "Gonna go make my special ice cream."

"Make ice cream?"

"Yep. Hope we got all the ingredients." She got to her feet and stomped her way into the kitchen. She knew she was behaving like a brat.

Fingers crossed he did something about it.

To her surprise, he did follow her into the kitchen. But that was only to watch her, arms crossed over his chest, resting back against the counter as she lined up her ingredients.

First, out came the tub of vanilla ice cream she'd bought a few days before this all went down. She ran some hot water in the sink then dropped it in to melt it slightly. Didn't have time to wait for it to melt on its own.

"What are you doing?"

"Making my special ice cream." Next, she lined up the other ingredients. Gummy bears. Mini Reese's pieces. Mini marshmallows. Chocolate-covered Turkish delight.

"What are you doing with all of that?"

"It's going in the ice-cream. Mix it all up, put it back in the freezer for a bit to refreeze. You can also put nuts and maraschino cherries in. You know, if you want to be healthy."

"I don't think maraschino cherries are considered healthy," he rumbled.

"They're a fruit, aren't they?"

He shook his head.

"Just you wait." She expected him to say something about all that sugar. Nothing. That unease grew in her gut.

He watched her assemble everything then pop it back in the freezer. "I'm gonna do some work while you watch the game."

"All right, baby," he said gently, kissing her forehead. "Got a surprise for you later."

"A surprise?"

"Yep. Be about two hours away, though."

Well, now she wasn't going to get much work done wondering about the surprise.

A FEW HOURS LATER, Jed placed his hands on her shoulders. "Time to finish up, baby. Your surprise is ready."

She saved the work she was editing. She stretched, aware of the nightie rising up. And the fact she wasn't wearing any panties. But his eyes didn't drop. He didn't pull her close and squeeze her ass with his huge hand.

He didn't want her anymore. Disappointment and regret blended together into a huge ball of pain as he took her hand. He wrapped the blanket he'd pulled off the sofa around her and led her outside onto the back porch.

Twilight was here. This was actually her favorite time of night. And she started to relax.

"What's the surprise?" she asked as he pulled her in front of him and wrapped his arms around her. Ooh, that was nice.

"Watch."

As the last of the sun faded, she watched with her mouth wide open as the trees around the house came to light. Lit with hundreds and hundreds of fairy lights.

"What. . .how. . ."

He rested his chin on the top of her head. "That asshole made you feel unsafe here. He watched you. This is your special place. I wanted to try to give it back."

Oh God, that had to be the kindest, sweetest thing anyone had ever done for her.

"Boys came and helped me while you napped," he explained how he'd managed this. "They pretty much bought all the lights they could find at Walmart. Came here with ladders, set up as much as they had time to do before you woke. Lucky you slept three hours."

"It's magical," she whispered. The day after everything happened with Moany Mike, a guy called Liam had come and installed a security system complete with cameras everywhere. She'd objected to the expense, but Jed had simply told her it was covered. When she'd asked Ellie about it, the other woman just told her it was all sorted.

This wasn't the same as the alarm or cameras. It was better.

"Want you to feel secure. Want you to have beautiful. To be happy."

She leaned into him, trying to hold back her tears and wished she could give him the same.

"DAISY?"

She avoided looking down at the concerned face on the laptop screen. Instead she paced back and forth across the dining room. She was trying to gather her thoughts.

"Daisy. You want to tell me what's on your mind?"

More pacing.

Molly was the bomb. She was amazing. Kent had called in some favors for her to get an appointment straight away

This was her fourth session and while she knew she had a long way to go, she hadn't pinched herself since that night Jed saw her thigh. She wasn't sure she wouldn't slip. And there had been a few times she'd really had to fight the urge. Those times, she'd used the techniques that Molly had given her.

No, it wasn't easy, but she would get there.

"Daisy? You kind of have to talk to me for this to work."

"He hasn't spanked me."

A moment of silence. She still didn't look at Molly. "Shit. I didn't mean to blurt that out. I mean. . ."

"You done anything to earn a spanking?" Molly asked.

Relief hit her. She knew Molly was in the lifestyle. That her husband was also her Dom. Still, they hadn't really talked about any of this.

"Plenty." She had too much nervous energy to sit. "I made myself my special ice cream, it's full of sugary treats. Stuff I'm not supposed to eat unless I have permission. I ate two big bowls of it right in front of him. I nearly made myself ill."

Her tummy had ached all night.

"I hid my binky. He doesn't like me sucking my thumb and I've done it every night for the last week." She took a deep breath, turned to Molly. "I hid the paddle."

Molly's eyes widened. "Jesus, girl."

"He hasn't said a word."

"Daisy—"

"He hasn't kissed me."

"What?"

"I mean, he kisses me on the forehead or a light peck on the lips. But he hasn't *kissed* me. He used to devour me with his eyes. Now I'm worried that all he sees when he looks at me is someone to pity. A victim."

She clenched her hands into fists, waiting for Molly to reply. The other woman looked thoughtful. "You've had ten years with this. He's had, what? A week?"

She nodded.

"And while you've got things to work through, so does he. Is he talking to anyone?"

"He said he would, but I don't think he has."

"From what you've told me, he's a protective man. Looks after those around him."

"Yes, he's my dragon."

Molly smiled at her. "Man like that, he's not going to take it well that you were hurt and he wasn't there to protect you. Even worse, it was done by someone he loved. Someone he trusted. Done to push the two of you apart."

She nodded. She knew Molly would get it.

"Man like that, he's protective and used to being in control. He's also not going to like that he had no idea you were being stalked. That once more, someone got to you and he wasn't there to protect you."

"Neither of those were his fault."

"No, but I bet he blames himself."

She nodded miserably. "What do I do? Do I give him time? Do I just wait?"

"Man like that, patience doesn't always work. I want to talk to him."

That wasn't what she'd expected.

"Uh, Molly. . ."

"Send him in. Give me ten minutes with him."

"Molly, I don't know—"

"Send him in, Daisy."

"Okay."

JED WASN'T QUITE sure why Molly wanted him in today's session, but if it would help Daisy, he would do what he had to do. He hated that she was still having nightmares. That at times he'd catch her just sitting and staring off into the distance.

It killed him. Not knowing how to help her.

He walked into the dining room. Normally, he made himself scarce upstairs to give them privacy.

"Afternoon, Jed," Molly said cheerfully.

"Molly. All good, baby?" he asked Daisy carefully.

She looked worried, but she nodded.

"Daisy, give us a few minutes, yeah? Jed will let you know when I'm ready for you again."

That was different. He'd only ever spoken to Molly with Daisy there. Daisy gave him a nervous smile, but left.

"What's wrong? Daisy okay?" he snapped at Molly.

"Would you like to tell me?" she replied calmly.

"You're her therapist."

"And you're her man, her Dom, her Daddy. What's your take on how she's doing?"

She wanted to get a feel for how Daisy was doing. He could do that. "Nightmares are getting better. Didn't have one at all last night. She still jumps at loud noises and sometimes I catch her staring into the distance and know she's thinking about it."

Molly nodded. "And with your relationship? How are things

going there?"

He narrowed her gaze. "Not sure that's any of your business."

"Your relationship plays a large role in Daisy's well-being. And yours."

"I'm not the one who needs your help."

"Don't you? Tell me, Jed. How are you sleeping?"

Like shit. But he wasn't telling her that. "I'll call Daisy back. Tell her we're finished." He turned away.

"She's worried you see her as a victim and you no longer desire her."

He froze. Turned. "What?"

"Normally, you understand, I wouldn't be able to tell you this. But Daisy knows I'm talking to you. She's worried about you. About her relationship with you."

"She can talk to me."

"You hadn't had long together before all of this hit, and you were just feeling your way with your relationship. Your roles. You were guiding that. Leading her. As you'd expect seeing as she had no idea about any of that. You know that a huge part of a relationship like this is communication, yeah?"

"Yeah." He had an uneasy feeling where she was going.

"You communicating with her? Telling her how you're feeling about all this? What's going through your mind?"

"I'm not laying that shit on her. She's been through enough."

"So have you."

"I'm not the one who was sexually assaulted and driven out of their home. Had to take care of my siblings, living on the bones of my ass. Wasn't the one targeted by a fucking stalker, who watched me while I undressed. Who sent me sick notes."

"No, but that doesn't mean it's not affecting you. My guess is you feel guilty."

He just sent her a look.

"Yeah, that's what I thought. You feel guilty over what

happened ten years ago. You feel like you should never have left her? That you should have dug deeper to find out why she left? Should have gone after her?"

He nodded. He felt all of that.

"Should have known she had a stalker? Have protected her better?"

Yep.

"Should have listened to her when she wanted to explain what happened back then? Should have never blamed her?"

He blanched.

"Yeah, mountain of guilt there. But, Jed, you have to figure out a way of letting that guilt go. You don't, it will eat you up and it will ruin your life. You want to do that to you? To her?"

"Of course I don't. But what the fuck am I supposed to do?"

"Talk to someone about it all. Let it out."

He breathed deep. Let it out.

"You might also want to pay attention to Daisy."

"I pay attention." He frowned. He hardly had his eyes off her.

"You might watch her but you're not paying attention. She knows what she wants. It's you. All of you. She got a taste of all that she's ever wanted and now you're holding that back. She's been trying to get your attention for days. When's the last time you saw her paddle? How many of your rules has she broken in the last few days?"

He thought that over.

"How many times you let her get away with breaking those rules?"

"She needs care," he growled.

"She does. What she doesn't need is someone treating her like she's broken. When was the last time you kissed her? Really kissed her? Showed her you desired her?"

"I don't want to scare her." He ran his hand over his face. "She's never been with anyone else."

"And that's a gift you'll need to be careful with. But I know you'll handle her gently. Do that, make it good for her, and let her help you get past this."

Christ. Had he really fucked this up so much?

"And for God's sake, will you give her the spanking she's so clearly asking for."

He gave her an incredulous look. "Really should have looked into your credentials."

"They're solid." She grinned. "Most people like my brand of therapy."

He grunted. She laughed. "All right, I've given you enough to think about. Go do what you gotta do and send Daisy in."

He shook his head, walked out of the dining room, towards the stairs. "Daisy-girl? Molly wants you."

She appeared at the top of the stairs, then started to race down them as she liked to do. He scowled.

"Slow down," he demanded, reaching out to grab her and lift her down the last few. Then he gave her a sharp smack on the ass. "I catch you running down the stairs like that again and you're gonna spend the day walking around with a plug in your ass. Let's see if that slows you down."

Her eyes widened. Then a smile crossed her face that was so large, so beautiful he felt it fill his heart. Yeah, Molly was right. She needed him. All of him.

And he needed to somehow get rid of this guilt.

"I'm gonna go call Bain." He gave her a brief kiss but this one was hard, with some tongue. When he stepped back, she was swaying. He started up the stairs, then stopped as he heard her whisper.

"Molly is a fricking miracle worker."

He didn't turn to look at her as he spoke, "Oh, and sugar?"

"Yes?"

"Afterwards, we're gonna have a chat about all the rules you've broken lately. Don't think I haven't noticed."

"Well, shit."

For the first time in a week he found himself grinning.

SHE REALLY DID NOT THINK this through well.

That was her thought as she stood between Jed's open legs. He was sitting on the sofa. She'd finished her session with Molly, then made them a quick dinner of burritos. Jed had come down some time later and she could tell almost straight away he was different. He was moving easier. There was still some way to go, of course. It wasn't an instant thing. But he walked straight over to her, pulled her into his arms and kissed her.

The kiss was hot. It was damned hot. Her nerve endings were still sizzling. And she hadn't been happy when he'd pulled back. But they'd sat and ate dinner. And it felt normal.

She so badly needed normal.

Which was crazy when you considered her life. After dinner, he'd cleaned up while he'd sent her upstairs, with a warning to walk not run, to put on her nightie and get ready for bed then meet him in the lounge. Considering it was only seven at night, she hadn't reacted well. She'd ended up receiving several smacks to her ass, before being sent upstairs to get ready.

And now here they were, her standing between his open legs, staring down into his stern face.

"Want you to know something, sugar."

She frowned slightly but nodded. "I may not be the easiest guy. May not be the most communicative. But I always want what's best for you. That's my job. To look after you. Give you what you need."

"I want to do that for you, too."

"I know you do. So you have to know you can come to me about anything."

She bit her lip. "Are you mad about me talking to Molly?"

He frowned. "Babe, she's your therapist."

"I mean, about us. You."

"Nope. Not mad. Not at you. Upset with myself because I didn't make it easy for you to come to me."

"You're hurting too." Maybe more than she was.

"Carrying a lot of guilt and anger, baby. Won't lie about that. It's not gonna go magically away. But I've had a lot of smart people give me a lot of good advice. Gonna start taking it."

She breathed out a sigh.

"We got to keep moving forward. You're doing that. I've got to as well."

Wait. Worry unfurled. "You don't want to move forward with me?"

His eyes flared open. "Fuck. Course I do."

She put a hand to her chest, breathed out a relieved sigh. "Oh crap. You scared me."

"Sorry, baby. Damn it. Mucking this up." He grasped her around the hips lightly. "We're moving forward together, Daisy-girl. From now on, it's me and you. Daisy and Jed."

"Sugar and the dragon," she murmured.

He grinned. "Yeah. And I just want you to know, if you ever need to tell me anything, you can. You need me to slow down, you tell me that. You get scared or unsure, I'm the first person you come to. Yeah?"

"Yes," she said with a smile. "I love you."

"Love you too, baby girl. So fucking much." He let go of her hips and leaned back. "So much, I can see now how I've been neglecting you."

Uh-oh.

"You been getting away with a lot of naughty behavior, little girl."

That tone of voice, those words. They put her right into the headspace he was obviously aiming for.

"Sorry, Daddy. Wipe the slate clean? Start again?" she asked hopefully.

He shook his head. "I'm afraid I just wouldn't be a good daddy if I let you get away with everything so easily."

Damn it.

"But I'll give you a chance. You have five minutes to find your paddle and your binky and bring them to me. For every minute over that, you get three spanks with the paddle."

Fuck. Fuck.

He tapped his watch. "Stopwatch is ready. And go."

She raced away and up the stairs. Shit. Shit. Where did she put that damn paddle?

"And that's ten with my hand for running up the stairs!" he yelled.

Well, shit.

She searched frantically for that damn paddle, pulling everything out of her wardrobe. Where was it? Finally, she remembered that she'd stuck it in a shoe box at the very back. She drew it out and grabbed it. Yes! Okay, she knew where the binky was. She tore into the bathroom, pulled open the cabinet then grabbed the jumbo-sized box of tampons. She figured it was a sure bet he wouldn't look there.

Mind you, maybe not. There didn't seem to be much that scared him off.

With both held in her hands, she tore down the passage, slowing as she got to the top of the stairs, since she didn't want to add to her punishment. Then walked quickly down and ran to him, practically chucking them both at him before she'd come to a stop. Luckily, he caught the paddle before it could hit him.

"Shit! Sorry!"

He looked at her, glanced at his stopwatch. "Eight minutes."

"Fuck."

"And another extra five with my hand for swearing."

"What? That's not fair."

"That makes fifteen with my hand and nine with the paddle."

"Nooo," she whined. "Can't I just do corner time for nine minutes?"

He snorted. "Like you could last nine minutes in the corner."

Yeah. He probably wasn't wrong about that.

Well, shit.

He patted his lap. "Let's get your punishment over with, sugar."

She climbed onto the sofa reluctantly then lay herself out over his lap. Her legs rested on one side of him, her body on the other and he made short work of drawing up her nightie.

He rubbed her bottom gently. Then smack! She jumped with a startled cry. He kept spanking her, though. "I'm sorry I haven't been giving you what you needed, sugar." Smack! Smack! Smack! "Been too busy in my own head." Smack! Smack! "Not acceptable." Smack! Smack! "So from now on, you can expect me to be paying very close attention."

He stopped the hand spanking and rubbed her bottom gently for a moment as she sobbed. Her bottom throbbed but it wasn't too bad. Still, she was starting to wonder why she'd said anything to Molly in the first place.

"Now, comes Daisy's naughty girl paddle. Want me to hold your hands? I don't want you reaching back and getting hurt."

She didn't point out the obvious. But she guessed she didn't want her hands hurting as well as her poor butt.

"Yes, please." She reached back and he held onto her wrists, pressing them gently into the small of her back.

"Remember your safe word?"

"Yes. It's fruit."

"First time using this paddle, isn't it, baby? I'm sure it won't be the last." With those ominous words, he smacked the paddle onto her ass.

She screeched.

Holy shit. Holy shit. Holy shit. That stung!

Another smack before she even managed to process the first one landing.

"Daddy, no!" she screamed, reaching back with her hands, unable to help herself. Her legs kicked as it landed again, twice, leaving fire in its wake.

Tears dripped down her cheeks now. Her poor ass throbbed. She couldn't take it.

Twice more. She wriggled, desperate to escape.

"Easy. Easy, sugar. Take a minute. Process. You need to use your safe word, baby girl?"

His voice wasn't impatient. It wasn't tinged with temper. Instead, it was low, soft and it brought her back to herself. She took stock. Yeah, her ass hurt. Yeah, she didn't want more. But this is what she had asked for. Even needed.

Already a weight was lifting off her. The tears easing the way for more to follow that cleansed.

"I'm all right, Daddy."

"My brave sugar. Three more."

These landed rapidly, barely giving her a chance to breathe and then she found herself moving. He lay down with her spread on top of him. Her nightie over her bare ass as she cried some more cleansing tears.

"That's it, baby. Let it all out. My girl. My good girl."

She wiped her face clumsily and he pushed away her hand gently, using the sleeve of his shirt to clean her up.

"Gonna have to wash that," she muttered. His chest moved up and down, shifting her around as he silently laughed.

"You good, baby girl?"

"I'm good, Daddy. You?"

He sighed. "I'm gonna get there. With your help."

20

Daisy lay on the couch, snuggled under a thick blanket. Not that she really needed it, seeing as Jed lay behind her and he created plenty of heat. But she liked this. Cuddling with him. It was normal in a way that she hadn't had much of in her life.

The last few weeks had been intense and crazy, wonderful and scary.

So yeah, normal was nice.

"What's this show called again?"

"Ally James Murder mysteries."

He grunted. She was lying dressed just in one of her nighties. He was wearing a pair of sweatpants and a tank-top since he declared it was a hundred degrees under the blanket, especially since she'd insisted he light the fire.

Since his talk with Molly and his subsequent manly chats with Bain, he'd started losing that haunted look. Stopped watching her so intently, as though he thought she might disappear if he stopped. He'd even worked a few days. Although no away trips and each time he worked, he brought her out to the ranch to visit with Ellie, Charlie and Abby. Which was awesome fun. Although they did tend to get in trouble together.

Like yesterday, when they'd decided to make ice cream sundaes. Right before dinner. She'd gotten her butt spanked when they'd got home.

But those ice cream sundaes had been delicious.

Next week, though, he was working the whole week and she was staying here. Or, at least, he hadn't mentioned taking her out to the ranch. She was starting to wonder if he was ever going to take her to his place, but she guessed that could wait.

He nuzzled her neck. They hadn't had sex yet. And that sucked because she was a giant bundle of sexual nerves.

"She needs a spanking," Jed said, gesturing towards the TV.

"She does not!"

"Yep. She does. If you went around putting yourself in dangerous situations like that, you'd be over my knee."

She rolled her eyes. "You just want an excuse to spank me."

"Don't need excuses, you give me plenty of reasons," he murmured against her neck. His hand ran down her side then slid up under her nightie. He pressed it against her lower stomach.

"Jed," she moaned as he kissed down her neck.

"Payback. Lit the fire you wanted. Lying under this hot-ass blanket. Watching some brat on TV chase down bad guys when she should leave it to the professionals. So, need some payback."

"Okay," she said breathlessly. Whatever he wanted.

"Put your leg up on my thigh."

She raised her top leg, pushed it back, resting it on his.

"That's a good girl. Now, you just keep yourself nice and still."

She tried to concentrate on the show, to not notice as he lightly pinched her nipple then tugged at it. How he cupped her breast. She tried to keep her breathing slow, to stop herself from moaning as he slid his hand down her stomach, closer to her mound.

"Jed..."

"Just watch the TV," he commanded.

That was freaking impossible. Especially as he cupped her mound then slid a finger through her juices, pressing it down on her swollen clit. Her hips arched forward, a low groan erupting from her.

"My girl is wet."

Fuck yes, she was.

"She wants me badly."

God yes, she did.

"My girl is going to come for me, isn't she? Come for her daddy."

Holy shit. Those words were like an electrical current straight to her clit. He circled the swollen bundle of nerves. How could she be so close already? Was it a world record to come with only a few flicks of his finger against her clit?

Then he drew his finger away.

"No!" she cried out.

"When Daddy asks a question, he expects an answer. Now you get five minutes of me playing without touching your clit."

Daddy was a big old meanie. His hand cupped one breast then his fingers played with her nipple, tweaking it, tugging at it. She wiggled, trying to press back against him.

"Please...please..."

"Take your punishment like a good girl."

She sobbed out a breath. This sucked. She'd rather have a spanking. By the time he had finished torturing her with pleasure, she was a mess. She couldn't even see the TV let alone focus. She was on fire. Wet. In need.

For him.

He placed his finger on her clit.

"Please, Daddy. Please make me come."

"Yes. Come for me. Come hard, baby girl. Let me hear you scream."

She bucked in his arms, falling apart. She felt wild. Her orgasm roared through her, stealing her breath then returning it in a rush as she screamed.

"That's my baby. Good girl. Good girl." His words started to penetrate minutes later and she realized they were moving. He was carrying her up the stairs.

"Jed?"

"Not making love to you the first time on the couch," he told her.

She tensed. "You're finally going to fuck me?"

He stilled. Looked down at her. "Not fucking, baby. Making love."

"Oh."

"Fucking will come later."

Her eyes widened.

"Your first time, we take it slow and gentle. I'm a big guy, you've never done this before. It will take some time to adjust. I'll lead, baby. But I'll take it at the pace you need to go, yeah?"

Those jitters that had been growing faded somewhat. She reached up and cupped his cheek as he set her on the bed. "You always know what to say to make me feel better."

He grinned down at her. "Good. Now, take off your nightie. I want to see my baby."

Her heart raced. She felt her cheeks growing warm even though he'd seen her naked before.

He raised an eyebrow. "You want to leave it on?"

"No, I guess not."

He ran his fingers through her hair. "You're the most beautiful thing I've ever laid eyes on. And you're mine. Forever. Got plenty of time to see you, if you need it on for a while to feel more comfortable then that's what we'll do." He winked at her. "But I'm getting naked."

"Oh goody." She climbed up the bed to settle against the head-board and clapped her hands. "Show me. Show me."

He burst into laughter and she grinned. She would never tire of that sound.

She watched hungrily as he stripped off his t-shirt. He was gorgeous. Fit. Muscular. With a six-pack that made her mouth water. His hands went to his belt. Off it came. She pressed her thighs together, her pussy growing slick and needy.

Dressed just in his boxers, he crawled onto the bed and lay along next to her. Leaning in, he kissed her. And those jitters completely melted away. He could kiss. And when he kissed her, she couldn't think of anything else.

"Fucking love kissing you. Cannot wait to kiss you in other places," he muttered as he dropped light kisses along her neck. "Your breasts. Your thighs. Your pussy."

Her breath caught. "You want to kiss me there?"

"Cannot wait to taste you. Bet you taste like you smell. Straw-berries and sugar."

That's why he called her sugar, because that was how she smelled? He slid his hand up the inside of her thigh, making her gasp.

"Spread for me, baby girl. Give me all of you." His hand rose further up her thigh. Her heart stuttered then beat faster. Harder. He cupped the heat of her.

"Wet. So wet for Daddy, aren't you?"

"Yes," she gasped out as he gently pressed his hand against her pussy.

"Do you want Daddy to lick you out, little girl? Want him to play with your clit? To taste you?"

Her whole body was on fire with his words, his touch.

"Sugar?" He withdrew his hand.

She grabbed at his wrist. "Please, don't stop."

He immediately returned his hand to her pussy, as he kissed

her. "I want you wild for me, babe. I want to hear every noise. Don't hold anything back. Holding back is not allowed."

That was good as she didn't think she could hold back even if she wanted to. He moved down the bed, settling himself between her legs. He pushed her nightie up over her hips and she started to feel silly for needing the protection when he'd already seen her naked. But that was before he knew what had happened to her.

It doesn't matter to him.

"Baby girl, what you thinking?"

"You think I'm hot."

He chuckled. "Ah, yeah, babe. Think that's pretty obvious. I think you're fucking gorgeous. Smart. Sweet. Sometimes a brat."

"Am not," she protested.

He kissed her inner thigh. "You totally are. And stubborn."

"You can stop anytime," she said mock-grumpily.

"And I love it all. All of you."

She sighed happily and then she reached for the bottom of her nightie and drew it up over her head. And was rewarded by the way his eyes heated. His gaze grew intense.

"Babe," was all he said. But he said a lot with that one word. All of it good. He rose up, his weight resting on his arms as he sucked one nipple into his mouth. She gasped, her hands rising to clasp hold of his biceps as he tugged at her nipple, licked it, suckled on it.

She shifted beneath him as waves of desire flooded her. He shifted to her other nipple, giving it equal attention. She ran her hands over his back, touching him everywhere she could, needing to give to him like he was giving to her.

"Baby, you are fucking gorgeous. All of you. Not an inch of you I don't want to explore." He kissed his way down her stomach. "But this part right here, where I most want to be in the world."

He parted the lips of her pussy and ran his tongue along the slit. She cried out, her hips bucking up.

"Yeah. Go wild, baby girl." He played with her, teased her, stroked her up to the edge of coming with the tip of his tongue against her clit then dropped back to run the flat of his tongue across her entrance. Her body shook. Sweat coated her body. She screamed as once more he dropped back.

"Don't stop!"

"Damn, you taste even better than I thought. Easy, baby."

"No. Not easy. I want it now!"

"Demanding thing. I like that." He pushed a finger slowly into her entrance. "So tight. Got to get you ready for me."

"I'm ready. I'm so ready."

"Easy. Easy, baby."

Her head shook back and forth and then his tongue started stroking her clit once more. Her orgasm rushed her, stealing her breath as she shook with her release. He slid up her body again, kissed along her jaw. She tried to catch her breath, clung to him tight, needing that closeness to anchor her.

Then he rolled them, surprising her. His mouth found hers again. Ravaged her. She tasted herself on him.

"Think I'm addicted to your taste, baby."

She smiled down at him. "Can I taste you?"

He raised an eyebrow. "Sure you're ready for that?"

"I won't be any good. I don't know what I'm doing, but I want to try if you'll teach me?"

"Teach you whatever you need to know. But babe, ain't much you need to know other than don't use your teeth, the tip is sensitive and handle my balls with care. Especially at the moment."

She kissed along his jaw. "Got it."

Slowly, she worked her way down his body. It was a work of art. And he thought she was gorgeous? She had nothing on him. Skin like silk. Yet his body was so hard. Strong. Even though she'd just come, she found herself getting turned on all over again just from touching him, tasting the saltiness of his skin.

When she reached his boxers, she pulled them off slowly. He raised his ass and she drew them down his legs. Then she took in all that was Jed Carson.

He. Was. Magnificent.

Her heart thumped crazily. How would she ever fit that inside her?

He gave a laugh. "So good for my ego."

She snorted. "Soon your head won't even make it through the doorway."

"Got that right, sugar. Now take hold of the shaft at the base. That's right. Hold me nice and firm. Good girl. Run your tongue along the tip."

She heard him groan, liked the sound of his arousal. Liked even more that she was the one turning him on. She threw herself wholeheartedly into giving him a blow job. Every murmured command was committed to memory. She sucked. She licked. She played very carefully with his balls. She was so engaged in what she was doing, she didn't even hear him calling her name. Didn't know he was calling a stop to it until he grabbed her, pulling her up his body.

He kissed her. Hard. Hot.

"I didn't want to stop," she moaned.

"Love that you love sucking my cock. But I want to be inside you when I come."

She licked her lips. "I did a good job?"

"I've never had better."

"That can't be true," she muttered.

He rolled them over until she was on her back. "Never had better. You showed me that you loved what you just did and you fucking threw yourself into it so much that you didn't even hear me when I tried to stop you. So yeah, best I've ever had."

Happiness filled her. "Oh."

He grinned. "Oh. But now, I'm fucking on fire and I don't know how the hell I'm gonna last longer than thirty seconds."

He reached over into the nightstand and drew out a condom, rolling it quickly onto his shaft. Then he returned to her, his cock nudged at her entrance as he kissed her. Her breath came in short pants as he sucked on her nipple. God, she liked that. Liked it a lot.

"My baby likes her nipples being sucked."

His baby certainly did.

He pushed slowly inside her. She bucked against him. She liked the feel of that. "Trying to take it easy, babe. Make this good for my girl. Be easier on me if you stayed still."

"Sorry," she said breathlessly. "I've just been waiting for this for a long, long time."

"Me too." He pushed further inside her. "Wrap your legs around me, sugar. Tell me if you need me to stop for a bit."

She didn't want him to stop. Sure, he was stretching her. He was a large guy and she was tight. But it also felt so good to have him finally there. Inside her. Claiming her.

Slowly, slowly he pressed forward. It was the most delicious sort of torment. She shook. Moaned.

"Easy, baby. Easy. Nearly there."

She could see the strain on his face and she kissed along his jaw, rubbing her hands along his back, trying to help him however she could. And then finally, he was there. Inside her.

Honey flowed. Her insides danced. Rock'n roll. That's what he was. He sent shivers through her when he spoke soft and gentle. When he was rough and hard, he made her want to sing. Or scream. But all of it was good. So damn good.

He paused above her. Stared down at her and the most wonderful smile crossed his face.

"My sugar."

She smiled back.

"My dragon."

And then he moved. She clung on tight. Held on for the ride and hoped like hell she was making it good for him. He kissed her. Held her close. Murmured to her in that soft voice she adored.

His breathing changed. There was a hitch. It grew faster. "Gonna come, baby girl. You're coming with me."

Come with him? She couldn't come again. Could she?

He rolled his hips and he brushed against her clit in a way that had her eyes widening.

"Oh."

"There it is." He grinned. Then he did it again. And again. Until her orgasm rushed through her. Dimly, she heard his shout of satisfaction, but she was too far gone. Swimming on a sea of pleasure. He rolled, arranging her on his chest. She slumped against him, trying to catch her breath, to find the energy to speak.

"That. Was. Magnificent."

She felt his chest move. Knew he was laughing at her. Didn't care.

"Yeah, babe. It certainly was."

She managed to raise her head to smile down at him. "It was good for you?"

"Best I've ever had."

"Oh. That's nice."

This time his laugh wasn't silent.

21

She swirled her tongue around the head of his cock then pressed the tip into the slit. She loved hearing him groan, hearing him say her name, loved that she gave him this much pleasure.

"Take me, baby girl. Take me in deep."

More than ready for that, she took him into her mouth, took as much of him as she could. Then she slowly slid her way back up. Down quickly. Up slowly.

Suddenly, he grabbed her. Pulled her off him.

"No," she groaned.

"Not coming in your mouth," he told her. "Turn around, on your knees, grasp hold of the headboard and don't let go."

She loved when he got all bossy in the bedroom. He pushed her legs apart then surged into her. He bit down lightly on the spot where her neck and shoulder met as she arched back into him with a cry. In and out. He pounded into her, drove her up higher.

"Come with me, baby," he commanded as he brushed his finger against her clit.

She shattered. She thrust back against him. Taking him as

deep as she could. And he gave as good as he got until he roared his release and followed her over.

They collapsed together before he rolled off her, pulling her in against him, her head to his chest, his hand rubbing her back.

"Good morning, sugar."

Oh, it certainly was.

Forty-five minutes later, she stepped into the kitchen to find him leaning against the counter, sipping his coffee. His head rose and he smiled at her. "Got your breakfast ready, baby."

She wrinkled her nose as she stared down at the oatmeal on the counter. He reached over and pulled her so her back rested against his front then he kissed her neck lightly. "Does Daddy need to feed his girl?"

Happiness filled her. "I'm a big girl, Daddy."

"Sometimes. And sometimes you're my little girl. And I know that look, you're thinking of a way you can pour that down the toilet."

She sighed. Sometimes it was hard to have a daddy who was so observant. Which is how she found herself sitting at the kitchen counter while Daddy spooned oatmeal into her mouth. Of course, he blew on each spoonful to make sure it wasn't too hot and occasionally he'd make choo-choo noises so that was fun.

When she was full, he wiped her face and hands gently. Then he kissed the tip of her nose. "My beautiful girl. Go brush your teeth. We're going for a ride out to the ranch."

Disappointment filled her. "You have to work?" She loved going to visit her friends at Sanctuary, but she thought she had him to herself today.

"Nope."

"Then why are we going to the ranch?"

"Taking you to see my place."

This was unexpected. She'd asked him why he hadn't shown

her his place when he'd brought her out to the ranch the other times and he'd told her it was having a few renovations.

"The renovations are finished?" she asked excitedly, bouncing up and down on her toes.

He grinned at her. "Pretty much. Come on, baby girl. Let's go."

SHE LOOKED up at the house with a growing sense of wonder. Jed parked and came around the front of the truck to lift her down. He was always doing stuff like that. Lifting her in and out of his truck, doing up her seatbelt. He treated her like she was precious. And she loved it.

"Daddy, it's amazing."

"You like it?"

She'd seen the other cabins at Sanctuary and they were nice. But this, this wasn't nice. It was magnificent. Constructed with logs, it had a huge, wide porch along the front. Complete with two rocking chairs that she knew she would make good use of.

"I love it. It's so beautiful."

"I saved up a lot of money over the years. Never had anything important to spend it on. Until now."

She smiled up at him.

"Didn't want to use the old bastard's money on this," he added. "Although I have decided what I'm going to use it for."

"You have?"

"Yeah. Gonna donate it to charity. Specifically, charities that help impoverished children and women who have been abused."

She blinked as she felt tears well. "I think that's an amazing idea."

He kissed her gently. "Come on, baby. Let me show you the inside."

It was just as magnificent as the outside. Large country kitchen with brand new appliances. A huge stone fireplace. And the big picturesque windows showcased the beauty of the landscape outside.

"Oh, it's amazing," she told him.

He gave her a soft smile. He did that much more now. Smiled. Laughed.

"This isn't even the best of it. Come upstairs. I have something up there for you."

"For me?"

"Yeah, baby girl. For you." He held her hand as he led her up the wide, gleaming stairs. He pointed to doors as they passed them. Master suite. Spare bedroom. Then there was a door at the end. He opened it and she walked into the room, her jaw dropping in wonder.

Dark carpet on the floor, covered in a pale green rug. Large window that looked out at the mountains beyond. A sleigh daybed with a pale green bedspread that matched the rug on the floor. In one corner there was a large, white armchair with a green throw over it.

The walls were all painted off-white except for the one the bed rested against. It had a mural of a castle resting on a clifftop. A princess with short dark hair stood at the foot of the castle and above her, looming over her, protecting her was a glorious dragon. It took her breath away. She walked closer.

"You did this?"

"Figured your dragon could always be watching over you. Even when he's not with you." He winked at her.

She smiled back. "It's the most beautiful thing I've ever seen. I can't believe you did this. Is it really all for me?"

"Wouldn't get a mural of a castle, princess and dragon painted on the wall if it was for anyone else."

He strode over to the armchair and picked up the stuffed dragon sitting there. "Also got this for you, baby girl."

She reached out and grasped hold. She hadn't had a stuffed toy in years, but he was soft and shiny and best of all, Daddy had given him to her.

He moved in behind her, pulling her back against his tummy and hugging her tight. "You like?"

"Like?" She stared around. "No, I don't like it. I love it. It's magical. Amazing."

"I wanted you to have a special place in your new home. Somewhere you could nestle in."

"My. . .my new home?" Did that mean what she thought it did? She turned in his arm to gape at him. "Does that mean you're asking me to move in with you?"

His grinned. "Shit, no. Not asking, baby girl. Not gonna take the risk of you saying no."

"I would never say no," she whispered.

"So it's a yes?"

Hell yes. "It's a yes."

He picked her up and twirled her around in the air with a whoop. She giggled and held onto his shoulders with her free arm, holding tight to both of her dragons. He kissed her and she melted into him. Hmm, maybe it would be a good idea for him to show her that master suite.

He drew back and looked down at stuffed toy in her arm. "So, what are you going to name him?"

She looked down at the slightly goofy looking, green dragon.

"I think I'll name him Prince Charming."

He threw his head back and burst into laughter.

EPILOGUE

She poked her tongue between her lips as she laid out the foundation for her pirate ship.

A plate was set down on the coffee table by her elbow, but she didn't look up. Had to get this just right. . .

"Sugar, time for a snack," Jed's deep rumble reached her.

She flicked her gaze over to the sandwich that he'd used a cookie cutter to cut into star shapes. He was always doing stuff like this. And she really got a kick out of this big, gruff guy cutting her sandwiches into shapes.

She wrinkled her nose as she noticed the whole wheat bread. "Daddy, the bread has seeds in it."

"I know. It's healthy for you."

She heaved a big sigh.

"Do we need to have a chat about your health again, little girl?" That rumble had grown deeper.

Nope. They did not need to have that chat again. Mostly because that chat ended up with her over his knee getting her bottom warmed. She snatched up one of the stars and took a bite.

Ham, cheese and mayo. Yum. Although she wouldn't tell Daddy that.

After he'd moved her into his house at Sanctuary, which hadn't been that long after he'd *shown* her his house at Sanctuary, he'd taken her to Doc to get a check-up.

What Doc lacked in bedside manners, he made up for in thoroughness. And he'd been none too pleased by her weight, her blood test results or the fact she hadn't been to a dentist in years.

Neither had Jed. Which had resulted in a trip to the dentist, where she'd had to sit on the chair with a hot bottom, because she had vehemently protested visiting the dentist, and in such a way that Jed had made use of her bad girl paddle once more. A bad girl paddle that now hung on the wall of her special Little girl bedroom. Which she loved. Her room that is. The paddle, not so much. Nor did she particularly like the naps Jed made her take daily. But she had to admit between the diet plan that Doc had created for her in order for her to slowly build up her health and all the rest she was getting, plus all this care and attention from Jed, she felt amazing.

Now, if she could just get rid of that paddle. . .

She'd lived here with Jed for six weeks now. She worked when he did, and when he was home, she spent a lot of time as Little Daisy. It was amazing to not have to worry about everything, not to make all the decisions. It was like she was getting a second chance at a childhood. Only this time, she had the world's best daddy and the sexiest hunk imaginable, who gave her amazing orgasms.

Yep. Life was sweet.

Mostly.

Jed had gone away for work three times since everything went down. Each time had been hard. She wasn't sure it would ever get easier. But at least at Sanctuary, she was protected. She had people checking on her and not just Ellie, Charlie and Abby. Kent came regularly too. As did Macca.

And, to her surprise, Bain.

"I'm good, Daddy," she replied after swallowing her mouthful. "Yum. You're the best daddy ever."

He rolled his eyes, but she saw the happiness fill his face. He looked down at her pirate ship. "Who knew when I bought this huge coffee table it would get filled with Legos."

She looked happily down at the masterpiece she was creating. It was a huge coffee table and most of it was taken up by her castle, pirate ship and dragons. Since he was the one who kept buying it for her, she knew he wasn't really complaining.

She leaned forward to get a piece of Lego and felt her short skirt hitch up. Jed had a rule about no panties in the house. He also liked to dress her in short skirts and dresses. She had to be careful when people were around not to bend over.

But when Jed was around, well, that was a whole other story.

She felt him sit on the sofa behind her before his hand ran up her thigh to cup her bottom. "Damn, that's a fucking nice sight."

She sighed happily as he pushed his hand between her legs to cup her pussy. Her clit started throbbing in reaction and then her phone rang.

Her tummy tightened. She knew that ringtone. And this brought her to the one lingering problem in her life. Her sister.

Jed sighed. His hand left her thigh and she jumped up to grab her phone. There was nothing like a conversation with Sylvie to pull her straight out of Little headspace.

"Hello? Sylvie?" Answering her sister's phone call shouldn't give her this feeling of dread.

She saw Jed cut his eyes to her. The skin around his mouth tightened. She knew how he felt about her family. He wasn't impressed that Bradley hardly ever replied to her emails and that Sylvie only contacted her when she wanted something.

"Daisy? Hi!" Sylvie said cheerfully. All right, so she wasn't starting off with some sob story, that was different. She relaxed slightly and realized her fingers were aching from holding onto her phone too tightly.

"Hey, Sylvie, how are you?" Maybe she was just calling to see how Daisy was. She hadn't actually told Sylvie any of the stuff that had happened with her stalker. Although she had sent her a text with her new address and telling her why she'd moved.

She hadn't heard anything back until now. Which still had the power to hurt her. But not as much as it once had. She'd found her place in life. She wasn't lost or alone anymore. She had Jed, but she also had everyone here. She'd made friends, built a life that wasn't centered around her brother and sister or what happened ten years ago.

"Good. Sort of."

Uh-oh.

"I got your message saying you're living with Jed. That's awesome."

"Yeah," she said dreamily as she smiled over at Jed. "It is awesome." This house was perfect. It was a home. But then anywhere with Jed would be home.

His eyes warmed. Although he didn't lose that watchfulness.

"Must be saving you some money in rent and stuff then, right?"

Actually, she hadn't had a conversation with Jed yet about money. Or what she was going to contribute to their household. Mostly because she was too chickenshit to bring it up. He wouldn't be happy to know there was something she wouldn't bring up with him about so she was going to have to talk about it soon.

But the times she'd tried to pay her way told her that there was the possibility he wouldn't be receptive to that.

"I don't know, why?" she asked.

Jed's gaze narrowed and he grew tense.

"It's just, Max asked me to go to Hawaii with him on vacation. Hawaii! How amazing is that? He's wonderful."

"Who's Max?" she asked, this being the first she'd heard of him.

"He's my boyfriend, of course," Sylvie replied, sounding annoyed as though she was supposed to know that despite the fact Sylvie rarely told her anything. "You would love him."

Right.

"How long you been dating him?" she asked.

"Three weeks. But it's like I've known him forever," Sylvie said defensively.

"Three weeks and he's asking you to go to Hawaii with him? Max moves fast."

"Don't be snippy, Daisy," Sylvie snapped.

She wasn't aware she was being snippy.

"So, can you lend me the money?"

"To go to Hawaii?" Daisy squeaked. Before she could say anything more, her phone was snatched from her hand.

"Hello, Sylvie? This is Jed."

She lunged for the phone but he swung away.

"Yes, that's right. No, your sister can't come to the phone."

She glared up at him. "Jed! Give me the phone back!"

"One minute, Sylvie." His only reply was to put his hand over the receiver then stare down at her calmly. "No."

No? No!

She glared up at him. He pointed to the couch behind her. "Sit back down. Your sister and I are overdue for a chat and I don't want to be interrupted."

"She's my sister. It's my phone. I want it back."

"No. Sit down."

"It's none of your business."

"It became my business when you became mine. She's your family, which means she's mine too. Or is that not how this works?"

She chewed her lip. Damn it. He had her there.

"I wasn't finished talking to her."

"Your conversation wasn't going anywhere good. I see something that's going to cause you pain or stress, it's my job to intervene. So, sit your bottom down and stay there or you can listen while standing in the corner and afterwards you'll be sitting on a very red bottom."

Ooh, he was infuriating sometimes! But she sat. She also crossed her arms over her chest and scowled at him to let him know she didn't appreciate his dictatorial behavior.

Damn man just looked amused. "Sorry about that, Sylvie. What's this about Hawaii? No, she can't come to the phone. I'm part of Daisy's life now. That means I'm part of yours. So, tell me about Hawaii."

She bit her lip. Sylvie didn't stand a chance when Jed used that voice.

"Uh-huh. How long you known this guy? You run a check on him? No? What's his last name?"

She knew that soon after he ended this call, Jed would have one of the guys run a check on Max.

"And you called your sister to tell her you were going?"

He was silent for a moment. She squirmed, feeling embarrassed and ashamed. Jed knew that her sister only called her when she wanted something. She blinked back tears.

"That the only reason you call? To ask your sister to fund a vacation with a guy you met three weeks ago?"

She winced, wondering what Sylvie would say to that.

"You got a job, right?" Jed asked. "Then you need to save up if you want to do things like that, right?"

More silence as Jed obviously listened to what Sylvie had to say.

"And your sister works hard for her money. You're an adult. She raised you from a kid, she's always gonna love you. Always gonna want you in her life, but it ain't up to her to bankroll your life. Especially for stupid shit like this."

Oh, crap.

"You got a real problem; you can call me. You want to call just to chat about your life or ask advice or shit like that, call your sister. You need money for something important, we'll figure out if we can help you. Together. But your days of calling and your sister sending you money because you think you need shit you don't are over. Time to take responsibility for your own life, doll."

Her mouth was open as she stared at him. She could not believe he was saying that to her sister. Fuck, Sylvie would be having a conniption.

"You think anyone ever paid your sister's way? She's worked hard all her life to take care of you and your brother, too hard. Like I said, we're always here. But you want to go to Hawaii, you find your own way there."

He ended the call and placed her phone up on the top of the bookcase that flanked the television. It rang. He ignored it.

"I cannot believe you did that." She stood up. "That was taking things too far. Even for you. She's my sister."

"She uses you."

She winced. Ouch. "She loves me."

He nodded and some of that hurt eased. "I'm sure she does. But she's gotten used to coming to you when she needs something and that has to change. You got a lot in you to give, but I've got to make sure you don't give so much there's nothing left for you." He sat and pulled her onto his lap.

He rubbed his hand up and down her back. "I'm gonna do what I have to in order to take care of you. Including when it comes to your family. No one hurts my baby girl."

She melted against him. "I love you, dragon."

He leaned in and kissed her. "I love you too, sugar."

ELLIE TOOK one look around Aunt Rose's house before following Bear out the door. He locked it and pocketed the key.

"I think Aunt Rose is still watching us. That she brought Daisy here for Jed."

Bear cut her a look but didn't say anything. He just took her hand and led her around the back.

"The security system is a good idea. And boy, these lights are pretty," she said, following behind him with a frown of surprise. "Bear? What's going on? Where are we going?"

He wasn't the biggest talker, but he was being a little odd. He walked into the middle of the yard, where you could see the trees twinkling around and to her surprise, he stopped and dropped to one knee.

Her heart thumped.

"Ellie. I know I don't always know what to say or how to say it, but I think you know by now how special you are. That you mean everything to me. I can't imagine life without you and I don't ever want to. What I want is for you to be mine in every way, so will you marry me, baby girl?" He reached into his pocket and drew out a ring. She couldn't see much beyond the fact it was a big diamond that glinted under the lights. She didn't really care what it looked like, though. All she knew was her big, gentle Bear was asking her to be his. Totally his.

And there was only one reply to that.

"Yes."

READY FOR A CHRISTMAS WEDDING? Read on for an excerpt. . .

EXCERPT FROM A MONTANA DADDIES CHRISTMAS

"I want you to have a fantastic time, baby girl and I know with what your girls have organized for you that you will. But I also want you to be safe while having that fun. So, while you might not have to follow some of your rules tonight, like going to bed on time, all safety rules apply. Understand?"

Her eyes filled with warmth. "Love you, Bear."

"Love you too, baby girl."

"I'll be good, I promise."

He snorted. "Don't go making promises you know you can't keep."

She giggled as he tickled her side. "Daddy!"

He set her down then gave her a heavy smack on the bottom.

"Ouch, Daddy!" she said as she rubbed her butt. He just shook his head, knowing it barely hurt through the layers of clothing she was wearing. He nabbed her bag once more and took a tight hold of her hand.

As they neared the big house, Kent pulled up. Kent sent a wave their way then walked around to the passenger door and lifted

Abby out of her car seat. He whispered something to her that made her smile up at him.

Happiness filled Bear. He liked it that his two closest friends had found their women. Charlie and Abby were perfect for Clint and Kent.

Another truck pulled up. Jed. Bear wasn't as close to him as the other guys. Jed usually kept to himself. But he was a good man and since he'd found Daisy, he was a happier man.

The two of them finding each other after so many years apart was pretty much a miracle. Ellie insisted that her Aunt Rose had something to do with it. And even though Aunt Rose had been gone a while now, well, Bear wasn't arguing with her.

Jed helped Daisy out then tucked her in against him, his hand pushed firmly into the pack pocket of her jeans. Daisy had a lot of walls up to keep herself from being hurt. Trust didn't come easy. He thought it was a tribute to Ellie, Charlie and Abby that she'd opened up enough to show them her Little.

He also figured Jed's unwavering love and attention had a lot to do with that too.

All right, enough with the mushy shit.

He gave Kent and Jed a nod as they grew close. Then he smiled down at Abby first then Daisy. "Ready for a party, girls?"

Abby nodded excitedly while Daisy sent him a small smile.

"Think the question should be, are we?" Kent said dryly as he wrapped his arm around Abby's shoulders and directed her towards the house. "Or at least are we ready for the aftermath tomorrow. Gonna be some tired, grumpy girls tomorrow."

"Nothing a hot bottom and a good nap won't fix," Jed said.

"Jed!" Daisy protested.

Bear winked down at Ellie, who grinned up at him.

Coming December 10th

Printed in Great Britain
by Amazon

25411482R00142